**'You don't believe in love, do you?'
she asked, and Louis laughed,
raking his fingers through his
hair.**

'I believe in lust, and I believe in marriage.'

'You mean marriage based on...what? How
can you base a marriage on lust? Lust doesn't
last.'

'But it's an enjoyable starting point, don't you
agree? Not that I've given much thought to
marriage one way or the other.'

Lizzy shifted awkwardly. She realised that her
legs were brushing against his, and she primly
angled her body away from him. When their
eyes met, she could see at a glance that he had
noted the shift and was amused by it. 'And
what happens when the lust fades away?'

'Oh, that's why it's so important to be practical
when it comes to getting married. A decent
business arrangement doesn't allow for any
nasty surprises. There's no such thing as the
perfect marriage, but there *is* such a thing as
the perfect

The perfec   tabbed
her. When   *ia*, she
was nowhe

THE POWERFUL AND THE PURE

When Beauty tames the brooding Beast…

From Mr Darcy to Heathcliff, the best romantic heroes have always been tall, dark and *dangerously* irresistible.

This year, indulge yourself as Modern™ Romance brings you four formidable men—the ultimate heroes. Untameable…or so they think!

The Powerful and the Pure

When Beauty tames the brooding Beast…

Coming soon in 2011—four timeless love stories from Modern™ Romance!

IN WANT
OF A WIFE?

BY
CATHY WILLIAMS

First published in Great Britain 2011
Harlequin Mills & Boon Limited,
Eton House, 18-24 Paradise Road, Richmond, Surrey TW9 1SR

© Cathy Williams 2011

ISBN: 978 0 263 88648 1

Harlequin Mills & Boon policy is to use papers that are natural, renewable and recyclable products and made from wood grown in sustainable forests. The logging and manufacturing process conform to the legal environmental regulations of the country of origin.

Printed and bound in Spain
by Litografia Rosés, S.A., Barcelona

Cathy Williams is originally from Trinidad, but has lived in England for a number of years. She currently has a house in Warwickshire, which she shares with her husband, Richard, her three daughters, Charlotte, Olivia and Emma, and their pet cat, Salem. She adores writing romantic fiction, and would love one of her girls to become a writer—although at the moment she is happy enough if they do their homework and agree not to bicker with one another!

CHAPTER ONE

Louis Christophe Jumeau slammed the door of the Range Rover and favoured it with a look of pure loathing. Really, he should have known better than to trust in a car-rental agency which proudly proclaimed that it was the only one around for fifty miles. Lack of healthy competition invariably equalled a third-rate service; he had been proved right. He should have arranged his own private transport. He could easily have used his helicopter and had one of his own top-of-the-range cars on standby to collect him from the airfield.

But he had wanted to check out the transport links for himself. Over-indulged, wealthy patrons would expect efficient links to Crossfeld House, should they decide to get there by train, as he had. And onwards by car—as he, unfortunately, had chosen to do.

He cursed fluently under his breath, flicked open his mobile and was rewarded with a robust 'no signal' sign.

Around him, in the darkening winter light, the countryside was desolate and unwelcoming. There was also the threat of snow in the air. It seemed to be an ongoing threat for the inhabitants of Scotland and one he would have taken more seriously had he been in possession of a crystal ball and predicted that his rental car—*none finer than this, sonny!*—would have taken its last breath on a desolate road in the Highlands some forty minutes away from his destination.

He rescued his coat from the back seat of the old Range

Rover and decided there and then that the one and only car-rental agency for fifty miles around would soon be facing stiff competition, or he would pull out of this particular investment fast enough to make the heads of its five desperate sellers spin.

Crossfeld House—an addition to his already bulging port-folio of boutique hotels around the world and country-house hotels across the UK—would be pleasing but was hardly essential. Its unique selling point as far as he was concerned was its golf course. It had been enthusiastically lauded for its 'challenging qualities', which he cynically interpreted as 'unkempt to the point of unplayable'.

But he would see for himself. If he ever made it to the place on foot.

He would also be in a position to conclusively sort that other little problem out.

He slung on his coat against the bitter December winds and began walking in the direction of the manor house, his mind moving along from the problem he could not currently solve—namely his lack of car—to the problem ahead of him which he most definitely intended to solve. To be precise, his friend's sudden infatuation with a girl who, from all descriptions, fitted neatly into the category of gold-digger. Even never having met her, Louis could recognise the type: too pretty, too poor and with a mother hell-bent on getting rid of her five offspring to the highest bidders.

His mouth curled into a smile of grim satisfaction at the prospect of showing up on the doorstep of the Sharp family. Nicholas might be rich and successful but he was also naive and way too trusting for his own good. Mother Sharp might be able to shuffle her pretty little daughter up for inspection and Nicholas—whose visits to Crossfeld House on the pretext of checking out the edifice had become ever more frequent—might well have ended up as compliant bait at the end of the hook. But he, Louis, wasn't born yesterday.

And Nicholas was nothing if not a lifelong friend whose honour and bank balance Louis had every intention of protecting.

Fully absorbed by his train of thought, he was only aware of the roar of a motorcycle when it was virtually on top of him. It pelted past him in a whirl of gravel, ripping apart the eerie silence of the countryside like a shriek within the hallowed walls of a cathedral and then spun around, decelerating so that the rider, dressed entirely in black with a matching shiny black helmet, could inspect him.

More than anything else, Louis was enraged by what he considered wildly reckless driving.

'Very clever,' he said with biting sarcasm, bearing down on the rider and standing intimidatingly close. 'Get your kicks that way, do you? Or do you think that this is your private race-track and you can ride this thing however fast you want?'

In the middle of reaching up to remove her helmet, Lizzy's hands stilled and then dropped to her sides.

Up close and personal, this guy was bigger, taller and looked a lot meaner than she had expected. Whilst she knew this part of the countryside like the back of her hand, along with everyone in it, she was still sharp enough to realise that she was in the company of a stranger and there was nothing within screaming distance to disturb the isolation of the landscape.

She couldn't make out the guy's face but his voice was like a whiplash, raising the hackles on her back and making her want to meet his attack head-on.

'I didn't have to stop for you.'

'Are you going to take that helmet off so that I can see who I'm dealing with?'

Alone on a dark road, surrounded by acres of barren isolation and staring down a man who looked as though he could snap her in half if he put his mind to it: the helmet was staying on. Let him think that he was dealing with another man. One with a high voice.

'Was that your car back there?'

'Very good, Sherlock.'

'I don't need to stay here and listen to this.' She gave a few warning revs of her engine and waited for his apology, which was not forthcoming.

Instead he stood back, folded his arms and gave her a long, speculative look. The rising moon caught the angle of his face and she drew her breath in sharply.

The man might be aristocratic, arrogant and high-handed, but he was beautiful. Black hair was blown back to reveal the harsh, arresting contours of a face that was shockingly perfect. His mouth was drawn in a tight, displeased line but it didn't take much imagination to realise that under different circumstances, it would be curving and sensuous.

'How old are you?' Louis asked suddenly. The question caught Lizzy unawares and for a few seconds she was silent, wondering where he was going with it.

'Why? What business is it of yours?'

'You're a kid, aren't you? That why you don't want to take the helmet off? Do your parents know that you're riding that thing like a bat out of hell, putting other people's lives in danger?'

'There's no one else out here except for you! Trust a tourist to break down,' she muttered. Prickles of angry, nervous perspiration shot through her. 'If you're going to tackle this part of the world, then you should know to do it in a more reliable vehicle.'

'You should try telling that to the crook who owns the car-rental company by the station.'

'Ah.' Fergus McGinty *could*, she admitted to herself, be a bit shifty when it came to outsiders renting his cars. And anyone opting for the one and only Range Rover would have been cheerfully taken for the proverbial ride. She doubted the thing had been serviced since the start of the century.

'Friend of yours, is he?' Increasingly ill tempered, Louis allowed a short pause to elapse. 'So he's bound to know the teenager on the big bike when I decide to report you to your parents... Which makes me think that you have no choice here but to graciously give me a ride to wherever it is I happen to be going. Either that, or you'll find yourself answering to the police for getting on that thing when you're under age.'

Lizzy was tempted to burst out laughing. Yes, she could see that the high tones of her voice might have led him crashing into the wrong impression, and it was pretty funny when you thought about it. But somehow she didn't think that this was the kind of man who would take very kindly to being laughed at. Something about the way he held himself made her think that, when there was any laughing to be done, he would be the one doing it at someone else's expense.

'You can't just leave that car there,' she objected, purely to be difficult.

Louis made an exaggerated show of looking around him before his glinting black eyes settled back on her, his reflection bouncing off the helmet. 'Why? Do you think there are people lurking behind the heather, waiting to steal it? Frankly, if anyone is stupid enough to break in and able to drive it away, then they're more than welcome. They would be doing the world at large a service.'

Lizzy shrugged. 'Where are you headed?'

'Climb off that machine and you'll find out.'

'Climb off? What are you talking about? I thought you said that *I* would be giving *you* a ride.'

'Did I say that? Must have been a crazy slip of the tongue. Why would I endanger my life by getting on the back of a motorcycle ridden by a kid who should be at home doing his homework?'

'I could leave you right here.'

'I really wouldn't consider that option if I were you.'

Lizzy recognised a threat when she heard one. 'Where are you going?' she repeated reluctantly. 'If it's out of my way, then you're going to have to wait here and I'll send someone out to fetch you.'

Louis almost laughed out loud at that. Send someone out to fetch him? For starters, he had had enough of the great Scottish countryside when seen at night from the perspective of a stranded driver. For another, he wouldn't put money on the odds of the boy doing his civic duty when it would be a lot easier to bike off into the night and get his own back for being taken down a peg or two by an outsider.

'Really? Well, we'll have to differ on that one. I'm going to Crossfeld House and you're coming with me.'

Crossfeld House! Lizzy froze.

'You know where that is, don't you?' Louis said impatiently. 'I can't imagine there are too many manor houses with golf courses in this part of the world.'

'I know where it is. Why are you going there?'

'Come again?'

'I just wondered why you were going there, because you can't stay there… It's, um, up for sale. I don't think they're renting out rooms any more. And if you've come to play golf then the course isn't that great. In fact, it's wrecked.'

'Is that a fact, now?' Louis looked narrowly at the slight figure dismounting the bike, standing back to let him get on. 'So I should leave my clubs in the car?'

'Definitely. Do you even know how to ride this?'

'You'll find out soon enough. Let's put it this way—I prefer to risk my neck at my own hands than at the hands of someone else.' He revved the engine and enjoyed the full-bodied sound of the throttle. It had been a long time since he had been on the seat of a motor bike. He had forgotten how free and powerful they could make you feel. It was going to be an enjoyable ride, especially when he intended to make full use of it by squeezing as much information out of his passenger as he possibly could. Communications with Nicholas had been frustratingly restricted to his friend singing the praises of the Sharp girl, interspersed with one or two essential facts and figures about the estate. But this lad obviously knew the area, was almost certain to know the Sharp family and who wasn't up for a bit of gossip? In a place like this, it was probably the mainstay of their existence!

'So,' Louis shouted encouragingly over the roar of the motorbike. 'If you know Crossfeld House, then you might know the chartered surveyor there…Nicholas Talbot?'

'Sort of…' Lizzy clung to him. He wasn't kitted out for riding a motorbike, but he had managed to hitch his coat up, and through it she could feel the muscularity of his body. He had clearly ridden a motorbike before; it was apparent from the ease with which he manoeuvred it. 'Why?'

'I'm here to supervise what he's been up to. He should have sent reports back about the state of the place, but his communications have been erratic.'

'Really? So, you're his boss?'

'In a manner of speaking.'

'You're checking up on him?' Lizzy demanded angrily. 'That's awful—Nicholas has been working *really* hard, actually!'

'So you know him?'

'*I* don't know him, but he's… It's a small town, put it that way, and Nicholas has become a very popular member of the community.'

'Has he, now? Made friends…?'

'I think he might be interested in one of the girls here, yes…' Lizzy said in a guarded voice, although she had to shout that information over the noise of the engine. She realised that she had yet to discover the name of the guy to whom she was clinging for dear life but, that said, at least she knew that he wasn't dangerous—at least, to *her*. But as for Nicholas, would he lose his job just because he hadn't filed daily reports to someone who was obviously a control freak?

'He did mention something of the sort.' Louis's voice was non-judgemental, encouraging, persuasive.

Lizzy grasped that and thought that she would make her excuses for Nicholas's absent-mindedness in reporting back to his master, because she knew that Nicholas would never make excuses for himself. He was too non-confrontational, too mild-mannered. He would probably stammer and stutter and thereby secure his own sacking, because the motorbike rider was just the sort of guy who sacked people. Or maybe he wasn't even responsible for actually doing the sacking. Far more likely was that he was an errand boy of sorts, someone sent to check out the situation.

'What did he say?' Lizzy asked tentatively. She noticed that she was no longer having to shout, which meant that he wasn't driving quite so fast now. The roads were slippery, unlit and treacherous unless you knew them.

'He fancies himself in love,' Louis said with a dry, cynical laugh; Lizzy was suffused with a wave of rampant hostility. Not that *she* saw love and marriage as the be all and end all of everything, but her sister did. Her sister was head over heels in love with Nicholas Talbot and she bristled at the notion that this perfect stranger saw fit to be contemptuous of a situation about which he clearly knew absolutely nothing.

'Oh yes?' she managed to say coldly.

'In love with someone who's after him for his money, I gather from reading between the lines.' No point beating around the bush. If the boy knew anything about what was happening in the town or village, even if he was too young to be really interested one way or another, then he would report back—and the warning would be sent out that Nicholas wasn't up for grabs.

Louis had had his fill of gold-diggers. He had been tar-geted at the age of nineteen, when he'd been too young to have known better, by a woman of twenty-five with whom he had fancied himself in love. Of course, the love had come to nothing, and neither had the memories.

When he thought back to Amber Newsome, her big blue eyes, her tears and the way she had convinced him that she was pregnant so that she could worm her way into an inheritance that was fast closing to her, he could feel every instinct for self-preservation ram into place inside him. She had captivated him with her self-assurance at a time when all the other girls at university had been playing games, and for a while he had enjoyed every second of what she had had to offer.

But then the time had come for moving on. He hadn't banked on the fact that she would not be prepared to let him go. He had not yet learnt that his vast inherited wealth was something that should be kept under wraps. He had paid the price: three months of stress, thinking that he would have to marry a woman he no longer loved for a child he thought she had conceived, only to accidentally discover that he had been duped by an expert.

And then, when he thought of his younger sister Giselle—and the way she had almost been conned by someone who had been close enough to the family to know better—every inclination in him to listen to garbage about love and romance shut down with the finality of a vault door slamming closed on the crown jewels.

Nicholas was less sceptical, and therefore all the more susceptible to anyone after him for his money.

'How do you know that?' Lizzy asked, her heart beating fast.

'I'm an expert when it comes to interpreting the sub-text,' Louis informed her. 'Ageing actress with five daughters who desperately wants them married off; it could almost be a cliché.' It went against the grain to confide in anyone, but in this instance it suited his purpose; he could feel from her silence that she knew the family in question, had views on them.

'You must have heard of them?' He invited coaxingly. 'The Sharp family?'

'It's a small town,' Lizzy muttered non-committally. In front of her, Louis allowed himself a little smile of success. 'Has… Has Nicholas—Mr, um, Talbot—told you all of this?'

'Like I said, I'm good at the sub-text.'

'And at prejudging other people as well, from the sounds of it,' she threw back without hesitation. 'You've never even met this Sharp family, but you've already made your mind up about them.' Up ahead she could see the first straggling houses that signified the outskirts of the town. In these parts land was not at a premium, and acres of fields could lie between the houses, but everyone still knew each other and the town was really quite vibrant, considering its size. Beyond the town lay the still, dark waters of one of the smaller lochs and to the left of the town, commanding a hill top, lay Crossfeld House.

Lizzy had never known it to be anything other than verging on derelict, although half-hearted attempts had been made over the years to try and bring it back to life. The current owners, however, were not locals. They were wealthy businessmen from Glasgow, all ardent golfers who had, so the rumour went, bought it on the spur of the moment and then promptly relegated it to the back burner because they hadn't reckoned on the time that would be required to fix it up. And so it had malingered, until three months ago when a buyer had been found.

'You need to take the next left.' Her voice was forced as she directed him on to Crossfeld House. 'And you'll have to go very slowly. The roads aren't in the finest condition.'

'And how far away do you live from the place?'

'There's no need to worry about me. I'm more than capable of finding my way home.'

Zooming around on a bike twice his size, Louis was in no doubt of that. For the first time since he had mounted the motorbike, he became fully aware of his surroundings. There was peace, he thought, and then there was the silence of pure solitude. This place definitely fell in the latter category. Personally, he could think of nothing worse than a prolonged stay in a town where finding a mobile-phone signal could be a challenge. But he was confident that there were a lot of people for whom this sort of thing would be just what the doctor ordered, people who found it relaxing to escape the daily grind of city life.

Golf had never been a sport that Louis found attractive; he preferred something that actually increased the heart rate. But, that said, there were vast numbers of golfers out there and he could begin to see that Crossfeld House might just turn into a gold mine. Had the ageing actress thought the same thing, and therefore set poor Nicholas within her sights for that reason? Was she aware that he wasn't the outright buyer of the property?

There were just one or two things that Louis felt would be advantageous to make clear before his unwitting passenger headed back with tales of the outsider.

'What do the people in the town think about the buy out of Crossfeld House?' He initiated the conversation via a circuitous route. He was genuinely curious, anyway.

'That it would be nice for the place to be renovated,' Lizzy told him coolly. 'It's been a bit of an eyesore for a long time. Course, there's nothing to say that it won't go the same way as it did before.'

'Meaning…?'

'Meaning that because someone has money doesn't mean that they're going to make a success of it.'

'Someone like Nicholas, you mean?'

'I don't know where you're going with this.'

'Nicholas isn't the buyer, as it happens,' Louis said casually. 'Although he *does* come from money. Which is doubtless why he's been targeted as a catch. The fact is, Nicholas is the

chartered surveyor up here to give the place a once-over—
make sure it's not going to collapse into a pile of rubble the
second the cheque's signed.'

'Who *are* you?'

'I'm astounded you haven't got round to asking me that
sooner.'

Lizzy thought that she hadn't got round to asking him that
sooner because she had been too busy disliking him.

'My name's Louis Jumeau, and I'm the guy bankrolling
this little venture.'

Wrapped round his muscular body, her hands balled into
little fists and her heartbeat quickened.

'Nicholas happens to be a very good friend of mine,' Louis
said mildly. 'We virtually grew up together. We may not be
alike, but anyone who knows us would tell you that I'm very
protective of him. I'm also much more clued up on gold-
diggers than he is.'

Just in time, the manor house was approaching; it was
a majestic sight. In the light of the moon, it dominated the
horizon—even if the cold light of day would unearth all its
woeful inadequacies. Around them, the golf course stretched,
swelling and dipping, a rolling sea of frozen black open landscape. That, too, would be revealed in all its glory come the
morning light, of that Louis had little doubt.

He was vastly experienced in the ways of property develop-
ment, even though it was only one of the many strings to his
bow, and a recently acquired interest at that. With an inherited
fortune behind him, he had nevertheless succeeded in making
his own mark on the world of finance, and at the age of barely
thirty had reached the enviable point from which he could
pick and choose where he decided to invest his money.

Which wasn't to say that he ever made the mistake of in-
vesting unwisely.

'Impressive building,' he murmured, slowing the motorbike
to a halt and spinning it gracefully to a complete stop.

'Yes. It is.' By her reckoning, she would be seeing Louis Jumeau far too soon for her liking. In the spirit of encouraging the blossoming romance between Rose and Nicholas, their mother—the dreaded Mrs Sharp, whom Louis would discover soon enough was her mother—had organised a dance at the town hall for all the local big wigs and some from further afield. Furthermore, Nicholas had imported his sisters, a small additional down side which Louis would discover soon enough.

Lizzy cringed at what had all the promise of being a nightmare evening. Her mother might not be a gold-digger but she was very upbeat about Rose getting married to someone who was financially secure. In fact, it was a pleasant fate she often wished for all her daughters. Lizzy's runaway imagination instantly foresaw all manner of tricky conversations should the man now dismounting her motorcycle catch even the slightest whiff of that.

Oh Lord! She had made the effort to return home all the way from London—had taken a whole week away from school so that she could meet the fabulous Nicholas, about whom she had heard everything there possibly was to know—and it was just her luck that her arrival coincided with a six-foot-two avenging angel on some mission of mercy to protect his gullible best friend from the claws of an unsuitable woman.

And he still had no idea who she was! Not that that was a situation that could continue for ever. The second he let it be known that an unknown motorbike rider had rescued him from the perils of a frozen Scottish countryside, her secret would be out. She had told positively everyone in her family that she couldn't wait to get back on her motorbike and enjoy the wide open spaces and the beautiful, never-ending silence so wildly different from the crowded streets of London.

Lizzy felt the urge to groan out loud.

'How long will it take you to get back to your house?' He turned to face her and she had that suffocating feeling again as she peered at the stunning angles of his face from behind the safety of her helmet.

For once the feisty spirit, the never-back-down attitude, deserted her, leaving her dry-mouthed and strangely unable to think clearly.

With a sigh of resignation, she reached up and began unbuckling the helmet.

'So you've finally decided to show yourself?' Louis said with biting sarcasm. 'Wise move. I would have found out who you were sooner or later anyway, but don't bother; I won't report you back to your parents for reckless speeding on that bike which is way too…' With his mind caught halfway between wondering how he was going to retrieve his possessions from the rented car several miles back, and speculating on the condition of what he would find inside the rambling manor house, he was one-hundred percent not prepared for the tumble of long dark hair that fell out of the helmet as it was finally unclasped and pulled off.

For once in his life Louis Christophe Jumeau was rendered utterly speechless. He had expected a teenage lad. Instead, standing in front of him, her head defiantly thrown back and her dark eyes glittering with unconcealed hostility, he found himself looking at a woman with fine, stubborn features, a full mouth, which at the moment was pursed in blatant disapproval, and the graceful, slender body of a dancer.

'You're not a boy.' He heard himself state the obvious.

'No.'

'You're a girl on a motorbike.'

'Yes. I happen to like motorbikes.'

'Why didn't you tell me sooner?' His tone was accusatory.

'Why should I? What difference would it have made?' A brisk gust of icy air made her shiver. 'Besides,' Lizzy continued, stoking the flames of her anger as she remembered the arrogance and contempt in his voice as he had made his sweeping generalisations about her family, 'I was interested to hear everything you had to say about your friend.'

For a fleeting second, Louis wondered whether this was the object of Nicholas's infatuation, but it was an idea he dismissed before it had time even to take root. Nicholas had waxed lyrical about a beautiful blonde, sweet tempered and gentle. On all counts, the woman standing in front of him failed to meet the bill.

'You know the woman, do you?'

Lizzy decided to evade that question for the moment. 'I know that you're the most arrogant, high-handed, *unbearable* person I have *ever* met in my whole life!' Her mother would kill her for saying that. Grace Sharp had been eagerly looking forward to the arrival of this man. She had heard a lot about him and—Lizzy was ashamed to admit even to herself—a lot about his fabulous wealth and legendary status. Alongside Nicholas, he was to be the glittering highlight of the carefully arranged dance—and the reason why so many people were coming, Lizzy suspected darkly.

'I don't believe I'm hearing this.'

'You've never met any of the people from here and yet you think it's okay to make lots of assumptions about them. You're a snob, Mr Jumeau, and I can't bear snobs!'

'*Mr Jumeau?* Surely we should be on first names at least, considering the circumstances? And maybe we should go inside to carry on this conversation. It's bitter out here.' Another frozen gust tossed her hair around her face, and he watched in some fascination as she pulled it back and twisted it into a long coil to hang over her shoulder.

He had never considered himself a judgemental sort, but he had to admit that preconceptions he'd been unaware of were being trampled underfoot. Why shouldn't a woman be on a motorbike—a reasonably powerful one, at that? Why shouldn't she enjoy the same feeling of freedom that he himself could remember enjoying years ago when he'd still been a university student? And why shouldn't she be able to speak her mind? Although, granted, this *did* afford him a slightly bigger problem.

'I don't think so,' Lizzy said tartly, momentarily sidetracked by his sudden change of tone. She folded her arms and glared at him.

'Fair enough.' He shrugged, and in the shadowy darkness she was aware of a shiver of apprehension racing like cold water down her spine at the menacing glitter in his dark eyes. 'You've just accused me of being a snob.'

'Which you are!'

'And I'm not sure that I appreciate that.' His eyes drifted to that full, defiant mouth. Under the leather jacket, the jeans and the mid-calf hiking boots, he couldn't make out her figure; it was no wonder that he had mistaken her for a boy. He wondered what she looked like out of the masculine garb, then he impatiently snapped back to the point at hand. He wasn't here to win a popularity contest. He was here to size up Crossfeld House, to see how much money it would cost to bring it up to scratch, and to put any aspiring fortune-hunters in their place. Whether the girl in front of him considered him a snob because of that was entirely beside the point.

Lizzy wanted to jeer at him, to make some disparaging remark about how men like him, born into wealth and privilege, weren't entitled to ride roughshod over people they considered their social inferiors. But she was mesmerised by the stark, angular beauty of his face. It kept making her lose her train of thought, which she hated. Out of all the girls in her family, she had always prided herself on being the level-headed one, the one who was least likely to pander to a man.

'That's not my problem,' she managed to tell him in a lofty voice.

'No, I don't suppose it is,' Louis countered smoothly. 'But, while we're on the subject of prejudices, maybe you might want to stop and think about your own.'

Lizzy's mouth fell open. 'Me, prejudiced? I'm the *least* prejudiced person on the face of the earth!'

'You've just accused me of being a snob. Yet you don't know me.'

Bright colour flamed her cheeks and she scrambled for something to say. 'You're right. It's bitter cold out here and I have to be getting home,' she eventually muttered in a stiff voice. 'You can find the local garage in the Yellow Pages and call them to get the car, or bring your stuff to the house or whatever. Do you have any idea how long you'll be staying here?'

A spark of hope ignited at the thought that his hideous experience at the hands of his broken-down car might spur him on to make a faster than anticipated return to city life; in which case, there would be no risk of her bumping into him again. But any such hope was squashed when he shot her a half-smile, leaving her in little doubt that he had read her mind and knew exactly what had been going through it.

'No idea.' He glanced over his shoulder to the brooding enormity of Crossfeld House. 'Who knows how long it'll take to go through every room in that place?'

'But...but surely you'll need to head back down to London? And Nicholas, isn't he the surveyor who would have already checked out all that stuff?'

'One can't be too careful.' He looked at her narrowly. 'Why? Are you scared that you might accidentally run into me again? It's a small place, as you've pointed out; steel yourself for the prospect. And, by the way, spread the news that I'm in town and I'll be keeping a sharp eye out for the Sharp woman and her brood of grasping harpies.' Louis had no idea what had propelled him to tack that on. He wasn't a believer in being overtly threatening; there was usually far more to be gained by being subtle.

'You can always tell them yourself when you see them at the dance you've been invited to,' Lizzy returned, head flung back. 'And, as for the brood of grasping harpies, you've already made yourself perfectly clear to one of them!'

'I beg your pardon?'

'Let me introduce myself.' Although her hand remained firmly where it was. 'My name's Elizabeth Sharp and Rose is my sister.'

CHAPTER TWO

'HE's awful. Arrogant, overbearing...' Lizzy yanked on one knee-high boot and glared at her reflection in the mirror. Lounging on the bed, fully dressed, fully made-up, and looking as though she had just stepped out from the centre of a magazine, Rose caught her eye and smiled.

'He can't be *that* bad. Nobody's *that* bad. Besides, he's Nicholas's friend and I know Nicholas would never have a friend who was as horrible as you say he is.'

'Why do you always give everyone the benefit of the doubt?' Lizzy grumbled good-naturedly. 'It's a terrible trait! Some people weren't born to be given the benefit of the doubt and Louis Jumeau is one of them.' She pulled on the other boot and made a quick mental comparison between herself and her older sister. Mental comparisons had become almost second nature ever since, at the age of fifteen, she had overheard her mother describing her to a friend as the odd one out. 'Too brainy,' Grace Sharp had lamented. 'And if only she'd do something about her appearance, take a leaf out of her sister's book...'

Where Rose was angelically pretty, with rosy cheeks, huge blue eyes and blond hair that fell in ringlets around a heart-shaped face, Lizzy was darker, more angular, more like her father in appearance. She had always made a point of turning a deaf ear to anything her mother had to say about the way she looked. She had fulfilled her brief as the clever one, fleeing to university as fast as she could; she had pursued a teaching career while Rose had stayed in Scotland and settled for working in a boutique in one of the bigger towns fifteen miles away.

From every perspective, they could not have been more different, but in spite of that they were close. If Louis Jumeau had made a point of telling her how loyal he was to his friend, then he had no idea how loyal she was to her sister—which was why she had kept quiet about the reasons for her animosity; not a word about gold-diggers. Rose would have been appalled to think that anyone could see her as the sort of girl who would chase a man for his money and, worse, she would have been hurt.

'You've gone all out with your clothes tonight, Liz.' Rose stood up, five feet ten inches of radiant beauty in a long-sleeved emerald-green dress and a little *faux* fur throw that matched her high black shoes. Lizzy didn't think that she had ever possessed any item of clothing in emerald green. She tended to stick to black and grey; it was impossible to be too much of a fashion disaster in blacks and greys. Bright colours she left for her sisters, who could pull them off a lot better than she ever could.

But tonight she had taken a leap of faith and borrowed a slim-fitting deep blue dress from her sister. The deep cowl neck showed just a hint of cleavage and made the most of her long, graceful neck. Her boots elevated her from a modest five-foot-four by at least four inches and, yes, she was wearing make-up: a light dusting of powder, blusher, mascara, eye shadow, lip gloss, most of which she had cadged from Maisie, who possessed enough make-up to open a small store.

'Have I?' Colour bloomed in her cheeks. 'I just thought that I'd save Mum from having a go. You know how she is…'

'Are you sure it's not because you want to impress the arrogant, overbearing Mr Jumeau?' Rose teased, smiling because she had noticed that faint flush on her sister's cheeks when she had casually described him as 'all-right looking, if you go for the tall, dark handsome cliché.'

'Don't be ridiculous!' But that weird, tingly feeling she had had two nights before when she had looked up at him was back. 'I could never be attracted to a man like him, Rose! I like kind, thoughtful men.' She thought of her most recent boyfriend, a five-month romance that had dwindled into friendship, which was probably where it should have stayed in the first place. He had been kind and thoughtful. Maybe too much so. Was that possible?

There was the sound of clattering up the stairs and then Maisie and Leigh laughing and talking over one another, while from somewhere else their father shouted at them to keep it down, that he didn't want complaints from the neighbours. It was a familiar routine. Maisie and Leigh were noisy and high-spirited, like puppies that had yet to be trained into good behaviour—although at least Vivian wasn't around to scowl and lecture, which usually had the effect of sending them into overdrive.

It felt strange, being back in the family home when she had become so accustomed to her own space, and she assumed that it was a feeling shared by all her sisters. Maisie and Leigh were on their holidays from university. Rose shared a flat with their old friend, Claudia, but from all accounts had been spending more time recently with her parents thanks to the fact that their house was closer to Crossfeld.

She should be enjoying the familiar hustle and bustle, but Louis Jumeau had unnerved her. She didn't like him; she hadn't appreciated his threats, she had nothing but scorn for his antiquated snobbishness, but she still hadn't been able to get him out of her mind.

'And stop looking at me like that.' She threw a cushion from her bed at Rose, and was relieved when the conversation was brought to an end by her mother threatening to leave without them unless they hurried.

The drive to the venue took half an hour. Six people piled into one reliable seven-seater which had seen off fifteen winters and was still going strong.

On the way, Grace Sharp could barely contain her excitement, while Lizzy stared through the window and tried to block out her mother's voice. She cringed at the breathless speculation about Louis and ignored her mother's demands for more information. Grace had revelled in Nicholas's attention to Rose. He was new to the area, he was wealthy and his family apparently owned a large estate somewhere in Berkshire. Could it have got any better?

Lizzy toyed with the entertaining thought of what would happen if Rose decided to dump him and run off with one of the hired help from Crossfeld House instead. Her mother, she suspected, would have a heart attack on the spot. But there was no chance of Rose doing that. She might have decided to play down how she felt, because she didn't want to make a fool of herself by throwing herself at a guy who might, just might, not be as serious about her as she was about him, but Lizzy knew that her sister was in love.

She surfaced to find that they had arrived. At once her stomach tightened and her mind, which had been pleasantly drifting this way and that, zoomed into the inevitability of seeing Louis Jumeau again.

The long drive was already lined with cars and, even as she played with the idea that she might just get away with avoiding Louis altogether by cunningly circulating in whichever circle of people happened to be furthest away from him, she stepped into the tiled hallway to find herself standing directly behind him.

Then, as several more people piled in behind her, eager to escape the ferocious cold outside, literally pushed into the back of him.

With a gasp of dismay, she tried and failed to right herself before he could spin around and find her clutching his jacket.

'Ah. So we meet again. And this time you're literally throwing yourself at me.' Louis had not been looking forward to this event, and already after five minutes it was living down to all his expectations. Lots of people were enthusiastically greeting Nicholas and were openly curious about the rest of his group, namely himself and Nicholas's two sisters—who, Louis had discovered as soon as he had poled up to Crossfeld House, had been invited to visit so that they could meet Rose Sharp.

'If you would just move on, you wouldn't be causing a pile-up,' Lizzy hissed under her breath. She felt hot and bothered and took a step sideways to avoid the crush of people arriving behind her.

'Are these events usually so well attended? Or are the local folk so desperate to meet the southerners that they're willing to brave Mother Nature for the experience?' He leant down, eyes drawn to the creamy smooth hint of cleavage. So this is what she looked like in a dress. He had to admit that he *had* wondered.

'You're unbearable.'

'So you've already told me. You're in danger of becoming repetitive.'

Lizzy chose not to answer. Instead, she swerved away from the entrance hall and made her way quickly and breathlessly towards the large room at the back which had been decked out with tables and chairs and a long trestle table which was manned by six girls, well positioned to spring into action the minute food was required.

Pausing by the door, she glanced over her shoulder and grimaced when she saw Louis looking at Rose, then at her family, who were introducing themselves, and then back at Rose. She could imagine the wheels in his head whirring around as he jumped to all sorts of conclusions.

The rise and fall of voices around her did little to calm her nerves, and not even the prospect of meeting some of her old gang could dispel the sickening knot in her stomach.

'He seems lovely.' Rose's voice from behind made her jump and she spun around and allowed herself to be led away to a quiet corner. 'I don't know why you were so worried!'

'He's pretending.'

'Don't be silly. Why would he do that? Have you met Nicholas's sisters, though?' She glanced quickly to the left and Lizzy followed her sister's eyes to where two tall blonde girls were looking around them with undisguised contempt. Whilst everyone had dressed up, they were in jeans and thick sweaters and were making no attempt to mingle.

'Have you spoken to them?' Lizzy asked anxiously, and she could see tears begin to gather in the corner of her sister's eyes.

'They hate me. I can tell from the way they spoke to me. Oh, they were very polite, but I just got the impression that they didn't think that I was good enough for their brother.'

'Nicholas is lucky to have you,' Lizzy said stoutly. She wondered whether Louis had infected them with his scepticism or whether they were all in a similar conspiracy of hunting down the worst-case scenario on Nicholas's behalf.

'Maybe. Or maybe he feels the same. Deep down.'

Out of the corner of her eye, Lizzy could see Louis looking around him. In a heartbeat of a second, their eyes tangled and then he was bearing down on them, cutting a swathe through the crowds, drink in hand.

'Speaking of Nicholas, why don't you go and see if you can find him…?' Lizzy murmured. 'Louis is coming towards us and I want to have a word with him.'

'What about? You won't say anything, will you?'

'Don't panic, Rose. You know how tactful I am.'

Now that she was looking at him approach, she found that she couldn't tear her eyes away. He, at least, had made an effort with his clothes: a dark suit which fitted so perfectly that it could only have been made to measure, and a white shirt, on which he had undone the top two buttons. It might be freezing outside but the place was warm, warm enough for everyone to have disposed of their coats, jackets, cardigans and scarves.

He was spectacularly good-looking, she reluctantly registered to herself, and he moved with the easy grace of an athlete. As he walked by, heads swung in his direction and a fair few of them lingered. Of course, he would know the effect he had on people. It was probably just one of the things that contributed to his arrogance. She rallied her fighting spirit at the thought of that and took a swig of her drink, white wine which had become tepid over the course of the hour.

'Are you having a good time?' She greeted him coolly when he was finally standing in front of her, affording her the sort of undiluted attention that made her pulses race.

Louis took his time answering. 'It's always illuminating to watch and observe.'

'Watch and observe? You mean in the way a scientist watches and observes bacteria on a Petri dish?'

'You're very different from your sisters.'

Lizzy's eyes narrowed. 'How so?'

'Well, your two younger ones are obviously party animals without a care in the world, and Rose…'

'What about Rose?'

'Very sweet-tempered, or at least that's the image she's trying to project.'

Lizzy bristled, but before she could jump in with a suitable retort he was talking again, his voice a low, lazy drawl, his incredibly dark eyes roving over her flushed, angry face.

'And your mother seems delighted with the fact that she's going out with Nicholas. In fact, I think she can hear wedding bells in the air… True or false?'

Lizzy tried not to grimace. Gracie Sharp had always aspired

to financial security. She had been the driving hand behind their father's work ethic, always pushing him to go a little further, do a little better and aim a little higher, and Lizzy could understand that. In fact, she could feel a grudging empathy, because her mother had grown up in a series of foster homes, relying on her looks to pull her through in the absence of any real education. She had duly chosen to launch herself into the world of acting, but it had been a struggle, and one she had from all accounts abandoned the day she had met their father. The legacy of poverty had lived on, however, so was it any wonder that she was now thrilled with Nicholas? At least one of her daughters was achieving what she had supposedly been born to achieve.

'All mothers can't help but think about their kids, um, finding happiness...' She wished he would move back a little, so that there was some chance their conversation would be interrupted. But his stance repelled anyone who might want to join them, broad back to the room, and she wondered whether it was deliberate.

'Really? She didn't seem all that bothered by the fact that there's no guy in *your* life.'

'You *asked* her about me? You were *prying* into my life behind my back?' Her eyes glittered with outrage and she clenched her fists as he returned her angry gaze calmly.

'There was no real need to pry,' Louis said with an elegant shrug. 'Your mother seems very forthcoming. I've heard all about your younger sisters and their hectic social lives, and Vivian and her causes, and Rose, who is apparently as close to perfection as any human being could reasonably aspire to be. And your mother just wishes that they would settle down with the right men. And then there's you—clever, ambitious— and there was no hint that finding the right man was on your mother's wish-list. Why do you think that was?'

Having watched and listened, Louis had reached certain conclusions, and conclusion number one was that he had been

one-hundred percent correct in his assumption that the Sharps
were fortune hunters. Everything backed him up, from Mrs
Sharp's obvious delight in her daughter's so-called match, to
Rose herself, who was the picture of gentle innocence, but who
was also seemingly lacking in the sort of passion he would
have expected to see in a woman in love.

He had made his way over to Lizzy because he had intended on pinning her to the wall. Inexplicably, he now found
himself distracted and, even more inexplicably, enjoying his
moment of distraction.

'I don't see that my private life is any of your business,'
Lizzy muttered, on the back foot and hating him for it.

'So how come you're not involved with anyone?' He swirled
his drink and then tossed his head back to finish the wine in
his glass. Just in case she got any ideas about going anywhere,
he reached out and planted his hand firmly on the wall so that
she was locked in.

Lizzy wondered how soon she could escape so that she
could strangle her overbearing mother.

'Repeat—none of your business.'

'A little tip—men don't like women who show their claws
the way you do.'

'I *show my claws* because I happen to loathe you!'

Louis laughed. He wondered if anyone had ever had the
audacity to tell him that they loathed him. Nope; he couldn't
think of a single instance.

'And,' Lizzy continued, fuming, 'I don't ask *you* about *your*
private life!'

'Ask on. What do you want to know?' He straightened, but
when he shifted it was only to further block any exit routes.

'I'm actually not at all interested. And anyway,' she couldn't
resist adding, 'I don't need to ask, because I can guess what
sort of private life you have.'

'Oh? Tell me. I'm all ears.'

'Lots of women,' she threw at him. 'Glamour models and

airheads who smile sweetly and do whatever you ask them to do. You have so much money that you can pick and choose, and rich men only ever pick stunning women. But my guess is that, when and if you ever do decide to tie the knot, it'll be with someone from your own class. That's why you don't like the thought of Nicholas with my sister. He comes from lots of money and therefore he should stick to his own kind.'

'You're flirting dangerously with my boundaries. And my patience.'

'You have been flirting dangerously with mine as well.' She looked at him and something wild and dangerous shifted inside her. Just as quickly she glanced away, but her pulses were racing and her heart was thumping so hard that she felt as though she might faint.

Behind him, she could hear the first strains of music as the small jazz band—two members of which she had gone to school with—began tuning their instruments.

'Care to dance?'

'You're kidding!'

Louis laughed again. He had intended to be brutal on this fact-finding mission, but he found that he was enjoying the way she scratched and bristled. It was novel. She had been dead-on target when she had said that the women he dated were beautiful airheads. Airheads didn't interrupt his work life, and his work life ate up a considerable amount of his time. She had also been dead on target when she had said that the woman he eventually chose would be someone of equal standing—no one who could possibly be interested in his vast wealth, which would mean that her connections would have to be similarly impeccable; no argument there. Neither type of woman would resemble the one currently nursing her empty wine glass and glaring up at him. A girl who got her kicks riding motorcycles and whose mother despaired of her settling down. Even in her finery, she still managed to have a slightly untamed air about her.

'Don't you dance?' he asked.

'I choose my dance partners with discretion.'

Louis made a show of looking around him. 'And anyone here take your fancy? Or do you go back too far with all of them? My guess is that familiarity can breed contempt in a place as small as this. Is that the reason you legged it down to London while your sisters stayed up here?'

'Rose is the only one who lives here. Leigh and Maisie are at university and Vivian is abroad.'

'Doing good works. Like I said, I already have the potted family history.'

'Isn't there *anything* my mother didn't tell you? Couldn't you just have chatted to her about the weather, like any normal person would have?' Lizzy blurted out in frustration and Louis grinned.

It was such a breathtaking ceasefire after hostilities that she felt her breath get trapped somewhere in her throat. The man was beyond good-looking, she thought in confusion. He was wickedly, sinfully devastating.

'I should mingle.' Her voice emerged a little unsteady and she cleared her throat. 'People are going to start wondering why we're closeted here on our own.'

'We're in full view of one and all. I doubt even the most imaginative could jump to any wrong conclusions.'

Which had the effect of immediately making her think of exactly what 'wrong conclusions' anyone might have in mind: which wasn't a comfortable thought.

'I can see Rose looking for me,' she mumbled, which wasn't a complete lie. 'And besides…' She sidled to one side and was relieved when he stood back, clearing a space for her, obviously as glad to see the back of her as she was to see the back of him.

'Besides…what?' His keen eyes took in the heightened colour in her cheeks and the stray strands of her chestnut-brown hair that were already disobeying orders and tangling about her face; she impatiently tucked them behind her ears.

'Besides.' Lizzy shot him a look from under her lashes. 'Nicholas's sister is beginning to get a little impatient. She's been glowering in this direction for the past fifteen minutes. I think she's waiting for you to wind up this conversation so that you can go and pay her some attention.' The leggy blonde had not moved from where she had been standing an hour before. Maybe she was just too deadly bored to move.

Louis frowned and glanced around him.

'I think,' she continued tartly, 'she looks a little jealous that you've been cooped up here with me. Are you and she an item?' Lizzy looked at Louis with an innocent, wide-eyed expression and wondered if she dared risk asking him how he liked the limelight being pointed in *his* direction. Judging from the shadow of intense discomfort that crossed his face, not a lot.

'You can't tell me that it's none of my business,' she tacked on swiftly before he could reply. 'You've spent all evening nosing into *my* private life, and it's only fair that I get the chance to do the same. So…are the two of you involved? Is that why she's here—to keep an eye on you?'

This was definitely well into the arena of overstepped boundaries. Louis didn't encourage any sort of intrusion into his private life by anyone, but where was his automatic response to slam shut the door in her face? 'If you're asking me whether I'm currently involved with someone, then the answer is no, although I'm at a loss to understand why you'd be interested in the first place.'

'I wasn't asking you if you were going out with someone! I was just pointing out that—'

'I had no idea that Jessica would be here. Or her sister Eloise, for that matter.'

'Well, they obviously share your low opinion of all of us.' Lizzy had now backed away to a safe distance and she felt some of her courage and fighting spirit being restored. 'Because they couldn't even be bothered to dress appropriately.' Her face was expressive of distaste.

Louis didn't say anything. The presence of Jessica at Crossfeld House was unfortunate. Over the past two years, she had been increasingly overt in her flirtations with him, despite his resounding lack of encouragement. And now he was forced to admit to a certain level of disgust at their blatant scorn for their surroundings. Louis didn't consider himself a snob. He was rich, he was careful and he was wary of gold-diggers. But Jessica and Eloise belonged to that category of spoiled rich kids who thought it was acceptable to sneer at people they considered lower down the pecking order. He had no time for them and even Nicholas, loyal brother that he was, privately despaired of their airs and graces.

'I quite agree,' he found himself saying, and she looked at him in surprise. 'It's rude, it's contemptuous and it's inexcusable.'

'You agree with me?'

'Why the shock? I'm a big guy. Maybe the box you're trying to cram me into is the wrong shape?'

'I don't think so!' Lizzy said tartly. She belatedly remembered some of the things he had said about her family. 'And now, if you'll excuse me…'

Food was about to be served and the voices had grown louder and heartier as alcohol began to have its loosening effect. She would have to go and stand guard by her mother's side. Her father would be drinking with his friends, and heaven only knew what other titbits of information her mother would come out with if she had more than a glass or two of wine.

After the enforced intimacy away from the crowd, every fibre of her body focused on Louis, Lizzy was forcibly struck by just how many people had made the effort to get to the bash. There were people from all walks of life; a lot she recognised, some she didn't.

Lizzy spotted Rose standing to one side, nervously sipping from her wine glass, trying to make some headway with Eloise, who was certainly the less obnoxious-looking of the sisters. Jessica had already been cornered by Louis and was talking and gesticulating to him, her beautiful mouth pursed into lines of sulky displeasure. She was being reprimanded! Lizzy realised with surprise. Louis's face was tight and disapproving and it was obvious that, wherever his loyalties lay, he had no qualms about putting Jessica firmly and soundly in her place. Lizzy had been happy to dismiss him as a narrow-minded snob, so how did *that* fit in with the convenient image?

With a little start of discomfort, she realised that she was watching the antics of Nicholas's sisters with just the same attitude of a scientist watching bacteria on a Petri dish—which she had earlier accused Louis of doing with her own family. So she spent the next couple of hours making a determined effort to talk and chat and absolutely avoid glancing in the direction of either Louis, Jessica or Eloise, or even Nicholas and her sister, for that matter.

It was after midnight when the place started thinning out. Adrian, her father, was beginning to look the worse for wear, and of her mother there was nothing to be seen.

'Where's Mum?' Lizzy weaved her way through the remaining clumps of people to tug her father away from his cronies.

'She left half an hour ago, with Rose and Nicholas. Apparently your Louis chap has acquired himself a driver and a proper car, or so he said, and he took Nicholas's sisters back to Crossfeld House.' Her father, angular and dark as she was—although taller and with less of a forceful appearance—cleared his throat and refused to meet her eye.

'Why? And he's not *my* Louis.'

'What did you think of the evening?'

'No good, Dad. Why did Mum leave early?'

'She wanted to help Rose pack an overnight bag.'

'For what? Why?'

'Rose is going to be spending the night at Crossfeld House. Ahem, your sisters have insisted on bringing home some of their friends, and there just wouldn't have been room in the car for all of us, and the house… Well, Rose volunteered her bedroom, and you know Maisie and Leigh…'

'I'm not following any of this. You mean you and Mum don't *mind* Rose being *together* with Nicholas at Crossfeld?'

'Times have moved on, Busy Lizzy, and you know Rose is a big girl now…'

'You weren't that liberal minded when Maisie brought home that boy from university last summer,' Lizzy reminded him sharply as her brain began whirring into action. It was unfair to try and pin her father down; she knew that. What her mother said tended to go, but she couldn't help herself. 'Tommy wasn't exactly suitable material, though, was he?' she speculated aloud. 'What with all those tattoos and the pony tail and the Student Union protests. But Nicholas… Mum *wants* Rose to go to Crossfeld House because she doesn't want Nicholas to have any kind of chance of getting away or of his sisters influencing him.'

'It's not that clear cut, poppet.'

Lizzy thought that it was a good job that Rose actually loved the guy. Would her mother have tried to railroad her into the relationship even if she hadn't? Would Rose have gone along with it because she was, essentially, so docile by nature?

She was struck by another thought. Shy, sweet-natured Rose was not the flamboyant or demonstrative type. Had it been Maisie or Leigh, the whole world would have known how they felt, and they would cheerfully have taken out a centre spread in the local newspaper to inform the few who didn't. But Rose was different. Did her mother want to push her daughter into cementing the relationship just in case Nicholas misinterpreted her shyness for indifference and walked away? Was a suitable match so important to them?

Her head was aching by the time Maisie, Leigh and their assorted friends were rounded up. And embedded in that hornet's nest was the spectre of Louis, watching, observing, speculating, assuming the worst.

Outside, a light dusting of snow had begun to fall. There was always an urgency to the weather in Scotland. What started as a dusting of snow could quickly escalate into a blizzard, and the prospect of that reduced even her high-spirited and very, very tipsy sisters and their friends to focus on gathering their belongings and getting home. Weary and confused, she decided that she would think about everything in the morning.

But the following morning she awoke to find that that tentative promise of a deterioration in the weather had indeed turned into a full-scale war of nature. The falling snow was thick and fast, and the sky was so dark that anyone would be excused for thinking that night had descended a few hours ahead of schedule.

Her father had made himself useful by clearing some of the mounting snow outside the house. Whilst the wind was so far making a nonsense of the snow stockpiling, it wouldn't be long before the countryside would be knee-deep in the white stuff.

Many a joyous day had been spent revelling in the vagaries of nature when she had been a kid. Heavy snow had usually meant days off school. Now, however, her heart sank. She could think of nothing else but Rose stuck at Crossfeld House, at the mercy of Nicholas's sisters and Louis, who would be circling her like a shark on the lookout for fresh blood.

By three o'clock, she was going stir crazy, and with the impetuousness that was part and parcel of her nature she announced to her parents that she had decided to go out for a quick spin on her bike.

'Just up to Crossfeld House,' she continued, backing away nervously from their duly horrified expressions. 'My bike's got fantastic wheels and I've ridden in conditions like these in the past.' *More or less.* 'I think Rose feels out of her depth.' A note of accusation crept into her voice, and she noted the shifty way her parents exchanged glances between themselves. But it was the tipping point, because her mother nodded wearily and then offered to prepare her a packed lunch.

'And don't forget your mobile phone.' Grace shouted up to her for the eighth time as Lizzy kitted herself out in suitable gear for the bike ride.

As if! But at least now she was doing something instead of sitting around, listening to her sisters and their friends play their music too loud, and spread themselves throughout the house with the easy indolence of nineteen- and twenty-year-olds who hadn't yet taken on any of life's little responsibilities.

It was bitter outside and the forecasters were warning of plummeting temperatures.

Lizzy revved the engine of her motorbike and felt that familiar thrill as it roared into life. She swung it out of the garage and down the short drive to the main road.

Three years ago, she had had special tyres put on that could better cope with snowy conditions, and she was now grateful for that window of foresight because conditions were truly terrible.

The trip to Crossfeld House on a clear, sunny day was a circuitous one of winding roads. Snow made the trip slower and much more difficult.

But it was only when the fall of snow began making it difficult for her to see that Lizzy eventually acknowledged that she might be in a spot of bother.

Ahead of her, the tiny pinpoints of lights from Crossfeld House at least indicated that she hadn't been totally disoriented by the blanket of snow. But those small dots of light were also a reminder that her marvellous wheels weren't quite so marvellous after all. And there was no way that she could *walk* the motorbike to Crossfeld; it was too big and too unwieldy.

Also, after nearly an hour of slow riding, the cold was beginning to worm its way through and under her layers of clothes, finding her tender skin and sinking its teeth in. Another hour and she would be putting her life at risk.

She pulled out the packed lunch which she had laughed at her mother for providing and gratefully bit into a cheese and pickle sandwich, washing it down with some coffee which had likewise been provided for her, despite her protests.

Then, with a sigh of defeat, she pulled out her mobile phone and dialled through to her sister.

CHAPTER THREE

LIZZY watched the headlights of the Range Rover draw closer, searching her out. This wasn't the tired old four-by-four which had been left by the side of the road. This was a shiny black monster and not much fancy guesswork was needed to figure out who was behind the steering wheel.

'You mustn't try and walk here!' Rose had exclaimed in horror when Lizzy had explained the situation to her on the phone. 'You'll collapse!'

'I'm not some kind of pathetic Victorian maiden,' Lizzy had been quick to point out, whilst acknowledging that her sister was right. There was no way she could walk to Crossfeld with the snow coming down in barrels and she was too far from her own house to risk turning back.

'I'm sure Louis wouldn't mind. He had a new car delivered; it would take him no time at all. Will you be okay waiting?'

'I *could* probably give it another try,' Lizzy had ventured optimistically, but the suggestion had fallen on deaf ears. Now as she waved to the car, making her presence known, she almost wished that she had pressed a bit harder.

'Are you completely mad?' Louis swung his long body out of the car, fighting against the brisk wind. 'What the hell possessed you to pull a stunt like this? Get in the car!'

Lizzy gritted her teeth together. Unlike the last time, when he had been on the receiving end of *her* help, he was dressed for the weather now. Thick jeans were tucked into black, fur-lined wellies and under the padded waterproof jacket she suspected that there were several layers of clothes. He was a fast learner.

'I can't leave my bike.' She folded her arms and stood her ground.

'And that would be because…?'

'It'll be ruined.'

'Tough. You should have thought of that before you decided to come haring out to Crossfeld House to rescue your sister. Who, by the way, doesn't need rescuing.' He flung open the passenger door. 'I'm giving you to the count of three, and if you're not in you can bed down here for the night.'

'You wouldn't dare!'

'If I were you, I wouldn't put that to the test. I was called out from an important conference call to rescue the damsel in distress. I'm not in the prettiest of moods.'

Lizzy climbed into the car. She should, of course, thank him for coming out to rescue her, but gratitude stuck in her throat; she stared ahead in stony silence.

'I'm sorry to have interrupted your conference call,' she eventually managed through stiff lips.

'You're a lunatic.'

'It's not the first time I've ridden my motorbike in snow.'

Louis glanced across at her. She was soaking wet, except for her hair, which she had managed to shove underneath the helmet. Not even the leather jacket, the boots and the scarf had protected her against the onslaught of the weather.

'I'm amazed your parents let you out of the house,' he gritted.

'I'm twenty-three. They couldn't very well stop me.'

'Which, of course, gives you the right to drive them out of their minds with worry?'

'Oh, please! I didn't think you cared about my parents *or* the state of their minds.' She shot him a sideways glare.

'You're headstrong. You're opinionated. You're arrogant.

And you shoot your mouth off without bothering to stop and think first. Little wonder that your mother's given up on your chances of marriage.'

Lizzy thought she would explode. She could feel herself beginning to hyperventilate with rage and she breathed in deeply, counting to ten.

'You're entitled to your opinions,' she said in a controlled voice. A brief silence pooled around them. 'I may be a little headstrong, and a little opinionated, but I certainly am *not* arrogant.'

'You were arrogant to think that your sister couldn't survive a night at Crossfeld without you storming in to her rescue.'

Lizzy squashed the surge of discomfort his remark provoked. Of course she hadn't been arrogant in thinking that she would be doing Rose a favour by showing up at Crossfeld to give her moral support; that was what sisters were all about. *But she didn't ask you,* a little voice whispered in her head. *If she had wanted your support, wouldn't she have* asked *for it?*

'Rose isn't like me,' Lizzy muttered. 'She isn't well equipped when it comes to looking out for herself. She gets upset easily and she never, ever fights back.'

'So you thought you'd jump on your motorbike and get to Crossfeld so that you could do her fighting for her.'

'What's wrong with looking out for the people you care about?'

'Nothing, but sometimes the people you care about are perfectly capable of looking out for themselves because they've moved on without you even realising it.'

'If you're telling me that Rose doesn't need me to look out for her then maybe you should see that Nicholas doesn't need *you* to look out for *him.*'

'You're right. Maybe he doesn't.'

He glanced sideways at her and her heart lurched as their eyes met in the silvery darkness.

'What are you saying?' Her heart was still in stop-start mode and her voice was high and breathless. 'That you accept Rose and Nicholas as an item?'

'I'm saying that I can't picture you being a teacher.' Louis moved the conversation swiftly along. What *had* he been saying—that he might be in the process of having a re-think because the bristly, outspoken woman next to him had managed to make him think outside the very tidy little box over which he had always had complete control? His mouth tightened in automatic rejection of that idea.

'Really. I mean, how do you cope with rebellious pupils without exploding? And I can't picture you wearing a suit to work.'

'A suit? Teachers don't wear *suits*!' But she couldn't help feeling hurt at the comment. He couldn't picture her wearing a suit because she didn't register as feminine as far as he was concerned. He had looked shocked to see her in a dress the night before. Did he think that her entire wardrobe was comprised of jeans, checked flannel shirts and leather jackets topped off by a black helmet and boots with lots of buckles?

'I love the kids,' she said brusquely. 'They're not complicated or judgemental and I can handle their high spirits. I'm in charge of the seven- and eight-year-olds—they're responsive and if they get a little over-excited I'm very good at dealing with it. And for your information,' she tacked on belatedly, 'I'm not a complete disaster when it comes to guys. In fact, there are some who don't like simpering women who only know how to say yes; some men happen to like women with opinions and ideas. And the reason I chose to come to Crossfeld was because Jessica and Eloise are snooty and horrible and I was afraid that they might be giving my sister a hard time. I figured she could do with a sympathetic shoulder.'

'From the looks of it, Nicholas is *extremely* sympathetic...'

'That's different,' Lizzy muttered. 'Besides, I wanted to get out of the house. Maisie and Leigh have friends over and they were driving me crazy.'

She stared out of the window and shivered, only suddenly realising just how cold she was and just how foolish it had been to get on that bike and think she could make it to Crossfeld in near-blizzard conditions.

She would phone her parents just as soon as she got to Crossfeld. They had never given the impression of ever having been worried about her. About her younger sisters, yes, because they had grown up getting into scrapes, and things had hardly improved, although the scrapes all seemed to involve boys now. And about Vivian, yes, because she was a do-gooder who always managed to find good things to do in very risky places and she didn't have the sense of humour to be able to laugh herself out of them. And of course about Rose, who was so placid that life and all its messiness seemed a constant threat. But about her, not really. Straddled between three stunningly pretty sisters and one extremely virtuous one, Lizzy had taken hold of the reins of independence from a very young age and had never let go.

Crossfeld House was now approaching, just an imposing blur through the densely falling snow.

'Is there a great deal of work to do on the place?' She broke the silence.

'Enough to keep a building crew very busy for at least a year,' he said, pulling up in front of the house as close as he could possibly get to the front door so as to avoid having to manoeuvre over the treacherous courtyard.

'Good Lord. That's going to cost a *fortune*!' she exclaimed involuntarily. 'And to think I shall probably have to dive into my paltry savings to get my bike repaired once it's been fished out of the snow drifts.'

'The repairs will be on me,' Louis said drily, wondering whether that was what she had been aiming at with her remark, but the look of horror she shot him was sufficient to tell him that he couldn't have been further from the truth.

'Don't be ridiculous. I would never, ever accept a single penny from you.' Lizzy opened the car door and slammed it behind her. 'And I hope you didn't think that I was fishing for hand-outs.' She folded her arms and stopped to glare at him.

'Accept the offer, Lizzy. If you felt that you had to come rushing over here for Rose, it was because of what I said, so in a peculiar way I'm partly to blame for the fact that your motorcycle is currently in the process of being buried under ten feet of snow. Besides—' he reached past her to insert his key in the lock of the rather grand oak door '—it's hardly as though it'll break the bank.'

'Thanks, but no thanks.'

'Well, suit yourself. But pride comes before a fall.'

'I've never believed in that old rubbish,' she retorted, stepping back. 'If I'm going to fall, I'm more than happy to fall with my pride keeping me company on the way down.'

Louis looked at her with sudden, vibrant appreciation and a flare of hot colour warmed her face. In the act of pushing open the door, he was so close to her that she could breathe in the woody, clean, masculine scent of him and it filled her head like an exotic, powerful incense.

She automatically stepped back, blinking like a mole suddenly exposed to bright light, then the door was opening and she was looking at the vast hall that she vaguely remembered from a thousand years ago.

Crossfeld House had been passed down the generations until its upkeep became too costly. Its glory had gradually faded, a grand old lady with no one rich enough or finally interested enough to give her the attention she deserved.

From what Lizzy could see, the place wasn't in bad order. The five-strong golfing conglomerate had obviously had high hopes of bringing it up to standard, but the plummeting economy had taken care of that dream, and in the intervening years jobs begun had not been completed so that there was an unfinished air about the place. There were too few paintings on the walls, the tired, faded wallpaper needed to be stripped off; one immense, high ceilings were dingy. But nothing could take away from the scale and grandeur of the place.

'Appreciate it while it's here,' Louis murmured drily as he followed her gaze. 'It won't be for long. The wiring's chaotic, and the plumbing has an agenda of its own, and by the time those two things get sorted there'll be nothing left of what you see.'

'It's a big task for, um, someone like you…' Lizzy said faintly.

'Someone like me?'

'A year out restoring this property—isn't that going to eat up lots of your valuable, high-powered time?'

'Ever heard of delegation?'

'You really do live in a different world from the rest of us, don't you?'

'Hence my natural caution about anyone aspiring to claw their way in through a back door.'

'Right. The gold-diggers.' She was comfortable being back on ground she understood. Just for a minute, when he had looked at her with that warm, amused appreciation, she had felt herself floundering, out of her depth and not knowing what to do about it. 'Where's Rose?'

'Safe and well,' Louis told her with infuriating amusement. 'And in the sitting room with Nicholas and his sisters.'

Feeling a fool, she trailed behind Louis, feigning great interest in her surroundings whilst wondering why she had come. They weren't about to feed Rose to the dogs. He had been right: she *had* been arrogant to assume that it was her sacred duty to watch over her sister like an unappointed guardian. When they finally reached the sitting room she could see from a glance that Rose wasn't cowering in a corner but sipping from a glass of wine and looking radiant in a pair of casual leggings and a long-sleeved grey jersey-top that promoted her fantastic figure without revealing anything at all.

She gave a screech of delight and rushed over, only to stand back and hold Lizzy by the shoulders.

'You're soaking wet!'

'That's the trouble with being stuck in snow.'

'Thank you so much, Louis, for rescuing her.'

'He didn't *rescue* me. He picked me up. I would have made it here just fine on my own, but it might have taken a little longer.'

Rose frowned and immediately Lizzy felt churlish and clamped her lips tightly together. 'Not that I'm not grateful. I am.'

'But what have you done with your motorbike?' Jessica demanded, standing up and tossing her long, poker-straight blond hair over her shoulder. She smirked; it was a glaringly obvious smirk even though no one else appeared to notice it.

'You look as though you've been dragged through a hedge backwards,' she continued, still smiling, still sounding sympathetic, but still looking at her narrowly, her bright blue eyes chips of ice. 'You should go have a bath. Or something. But I'm not sure what you would change into... You're a tiny little thing, aren't you?'

'Good things always come in small packages!' Nicholas exclaimed, joining in the general fuss and trying to smooth over the jagged undertones. 'Except in the case of Rose.'

'Are you saying that I'm fat?' She looked over her shoulder and laughed, and Lizzy was again struck by the idiocy of trekking her way to Crossfeld to help shore up the defences of the Sharp family. Rose was relaxed and more than capable of holding her own against Jessica and Eloise in her own quiet, unflappable way.

While Lizzy, the cynosure of all eyes, dripped onto the

carpet and mentally tried to figure out how much this little excursion would set her back in repair bills to her motorbike.

'I'll take you up to…which room, Nicholas?' Rose apologised, turning to Lizzy. 'Some of them are horrid, plus unheated. You could have my room. I'm…um…you know.' She pinkened and shot Nicholas an anxious glance.

'Wherever,' Lizzy muttered, only to hear Louis commandeer the situation by offering to show her to one of the bedroom suites which were on the right side of the house. The wrong side, apparently, contained rooms that were sealed off, ready and waiting for the plumbers and electricians to wreak their havoc.

'Don't be silly, Lou!' Jessica stepped forward quickly. This close, the comparison between them was even more dramatic: Lizzy still in her biker gear, wet and bedraggled, next to Jessica who was in a silky lounging outfit and a long cardigan that would have looked dreary on anyone fatter, shorter or less good-looking. 'I'm sure the poor thing already feels like an imposition without having you put yourself out even more.'

'The *poor thing*,' Louis said coolly, 'is more than capable of speaking for herself, Jessica. And the *poor thing* may have been a fool to contemplate taking a motorbike out in these sorts of conditions, but it's a damn sight more admirable than hunkering down in front of a fire, moaning about the cold and refusing to step one dainty foot outside the house.'

A deathly silence greeted this flatly dismissive statement of fact. Eloise giggled, while Jessica went white before spinning round to deliver a withering look at her sister.

'I *thought*,' Jessica blustered, crossing her arms, 'you liked women who looked like women.'

'Oh, believe me, I do.' The dark huskiness of his voice combined with the speculative, brooding look he shot her made Lizzy's toes curl and sent her thoughts whirling chaotically in her head. Suddenly the occupants of the room seemed to disappear, leaving just the two of them and the intense electric charge vibrating between them like a live current.

'Rose will be fine showing me up to a room somewhere,' she croaked. 'No matter the size or condition. We bikers are a hardy lot.'

Out of the corner of her eye, Lizzy registered Nicholas's curious eyes on them, while Eloise dived back behind the magazine she had been reading and Jessica pursed her lips together in rage.

Thankfully, Rose seemed oblivious. She was in her own little world with Nicholas, scared that it might not work out but deliriously happy. Upstairs Lizzy listened to her chatter away as she sat on the bed while Lizzy had a long, lazy, very hot bath with the door slightly ajar. She replayed that look Louis had given her, and the way he had shot Jessica down in flames without turning a hair. The more she saw of him, the less he corresponded with the one-dimensional image in her head—and, worse, he *interested* her. Just being in his company made her feel sickeningly alive, and not even submerging herself underneath the water could clear her head.

'And they're not too bad,' Rose confessed as Lizzy decked herself out in borrowed clothes, rolling the waistband of the trousers to shorten them, just as she had done with her school skirt when she had been a teenager, and feeling a little awkward in the skin-tight jersey-top. Her shoes were drying out by the radiator and, having refused to be seen dead in the fluffy bedroom slippers Rose had brought with her, she opted for a pair of socks.

'I mean, Jessica's a bit sarcastic now and again, but I just ignore her—and Eloise is a dream.'

So all was joy in paradise, Lizzy thought to herself. Even if *she* was more than aware of the snide digs from Jessica for the remainder of the evening, underneath the polite conversation. Malicious asides were camouflaged behind wide, innocent eyes; the little attempts to make sure that the conversation was dragged round to the subject of background so that she could chat about her privileged upbringing with the riding lessons and skiing holidays. Then she would ask, leaning forward with an earnest, kind, curious expression, what *they* had done for fun when they were kids.

From the sidelines Louis, sprawled after dinner with a cup of coffee, watched and said very little until Lizzy asked, twisting to look at him, 'And aren't you going to tell us all about *your* fabulous background and marvellous holidays? I mean, you've heard all about our trips to the seaside and camping excursions—'

'Which were wonderful,' Rose interposed quickly, snuggling into the crook of Nicholas's arm.

Lizzy wondered whether either of them was actually paying a scrap of attention to the conversation. Had Rose even noticed the catty way Jessica had managed her put-downs? The airy wave of the hand when she had dropped names and spoke of 'Daddy buying this' and 'Daddy buying that'? The sly, sideways glance at Louis and the quiet insertion of 'you poor things' when Lizzy had admitted that, no, they had never been on safari or gone snorkelling in the Bahamas? Nor had any of them had the privilege of going to private schools, never mind the boarding schools both Eloise and Jessica had attended and which—Lizzy had learned in too much detail—had been an *absolute hoot*.

No, Rose was in a world of her own, smiling and murmuring to Nicholas while he played with her vanilla-blond hair and twirled curly strands between his fingers. Rose most definitely did not need her assistance. Rose didn't need *anyone's* assistance. She was perfectly capable of looking out for herself by dint of a personality with a highly developed talent for denial.

'Oh, Louis was always the envy of our group.' Jessica had kicked off her flats and her long legs were draped over the arm of the chair.

'You mean you had even more fabulous and mind-boggling holidays than Jessica's safaris and yachting down the Grenadines?'

Dark eyes rested on Lizzy's face and his mouth curved into a slow smile. 'It's not the quality of the holiday,' he murmured, ignoring Jessica completely. 'It's the quality of the people you go with—and believe me when I tell you that I have never been more bored than when I was in Mustique, despite the turquoise water and white sand.'

Lizzy didn't believe him and, judging from the look on her face, neither did Jessica. Her head was beginning to hurt.

Did she really want to continue listening to never-ending descriptions of a life to which membership started with a price tag of a million pounds? No. Did she now want to have it rammed home to her just how much she and her family did not belong with these birds of paradise who lived their marvellous lives in this gilded cage? Definitely not. She yawned widely and stood up; Louis drawled lazily, 'Surely you're not heading up already?'

'The poor thing's probably exhausted from her escapades in the snow.' Jessica sprang to her feet. 'No, don't you move a muscle, Rose! I'll show Lizzy up. She's in the Blue Room, right? I need to get something from upstairs anyway.'

Did Lizzy believe that for a second? No. And, as soon as Jessica had shut the door behind them, she was proved right.

'How long are you planning on staying?'

Now that they were no longer in the sitting room, the act was comprehensively dropped.

'I'll be gone in the morning,' Lizzy said with equal bluntness.

'I mean from *here*. Back to London. Don't you have a bunch of kiddies back at some school or other? Rose said that you could only get a few days off and that you won't be back for Christmas.'

'I don't think that my movements are your concern.'

'True.' They were halfway up the grand, winding staircase and Jessica skipped up a couple of steps and then turned to look down on Lizzy. 'But you'd be doing yourself a favour by clearing off. All that business of Louis coming to rescue you; I wasn't born yesterday. I know every trick in the trade when it comes to getting a man, especially a man like Louis.'

'Sorry?'

'The unnecessary trip to Crossfeld? The stranded motorbike? The SOS call to your sister? You can flutter your eyelashes all you want at Louis, but you'd be wasting your time, and you can think of that as a friendly piece of advice. He would never look at you in a million years. He's choosy when it comes to the women he dates, and a little bit of bored flirting doesn't mean that he's actually interested.'

'I have no idea why you're telling me all of this,' Lizzy said coldly. 'Louis Jumeau is the last man on earth I'd ever be interested in. He's not my type and I'm not turned on by the size of someone's bank balance. In fact, it's a disadvantage.' Her throbbing head was making her feel giddy and nauseous. She clutched the banister and tried to focus. 'You're welcome to him,' she added for good measure, and the tinkle of Jessica's delighted laugh sent a spasm of pain shooting through her head.

'Oh, goody—I'm thrilled we understand each other! Now, you go up to bed. You're really beginning to look a little green around the gills. All that wind and snow can't be good for a girl; does terrible things to the complexion, you know…'

The following morning, Lizzy knew that she was somewhat more than just green around the gills. She was burning up, could barely get out of bed and her legs felt like jelly.

Rose came in and was a hovering, worried presence that she was fleetingly aware of before she fell back asleep.

When she next opened her eyes it was to find thin winter

sunlight trying to penetrate the thick curtains; a glance at her watch told her that it was after eleven. The banging in her head had eased but had been replaced by a general, shaky weakness that made a nonsense of her urgent desire to get out of bed.

In the middle of trying to manoeuvre her legs into obedience, she was hardly aware of the bedroom door being pushed open, and the sound of Louis's voice sent a shock wave of panic through her.

'What are you doing here?' Instead of being sharply authoritative, her voice was a feeble croak. She cleared her throat and fell back onto the pillow, pulling the quilt up to her neck and closing her eyes to block out the alarming sight of him striding across the room to look down at her.

'I'm doing my medical rounds. If you'd woken up half an hour earlier you would have found your sister doing hers. You've been out of it for nearly twelve hours.'

Lizzy cautiously opened her eyes and squinted up at him. He wasn't even a permanent resident of Crossfeld House and he already looked like a lord of the manor in a thick, checked shirt which he had cuffed to the elbow and a pair of faded black jeans that rode low on his hips. He was a man accustomed to giving orders, and he looked every inch the part.

'I was tired.'

'You're ill.'

'I'm not ill! I'm *never* ill. Rose has always been the fragile one in the family. Ask anyone. *I'm* as strong as an ox.'

'There's no way a doctor can come out here. You could say that we're snowed in, so you're going to have to rely on medication and plenty of fluids to get you through this bug you've picked up.'

Lizzy groaned. The word 'imposition', which Jessica had used the night before, reared its ugly head.

'We can't be snowed in.'

'You can't be ill. We can't be snowed in. Wrong on both counts, unfortunately.' Louis walked across to the curtains and yanked them open to reveal a continuing and dramatic fall of snow. 'It should ease by nightfall, if the weather forecast is anything to go by, but before you start thinking about leaving you might as well forget it. You're going nowhere until you're back on your feet. The last thing I need is for you to end up in hospital because I've dispatched you before time.'

'Oh, thank you very much for your concern,' Lizzy muttered under her breath.

'I'm going to send you up some food. What would you like?'

'Are you going to prepare it with your own fair hands?'

Louis grinned and lounged against the window sill with his arms folded. 'Would you enjoy it more if I did?'

'No, I would not.' Drowsy eyes took in the length of his muscular legs and the way his broad chest tapered to slim hips. 'I'd be scared you might chuck some arsenic in just for good measure.' Again she felt that shivery, thrilling feeling, the same tingly feeling she had had when their mutual animosity had suddenly vanished, leaving a charged electricity between them.

'I have to get back to school.' She changed the subject abruptly, although she was finding it difficult to tear her eyes away from him.

'Your sister's telephoned them to warn them that you might have to take a leave of absence for what remains of the term.'

'I have stuff to do in London.' Lizzy made an attempt to struggle into a sitting position but her body fought against any such show of strength. 'I hadn't even planned on being in Scotland over Christmas!'

'No?' Louis's ears pricked up at that. 'Someone in London you have to be with?' He played with the idea of her with a man and dismissed the crazy idea that he didn't much like it. 'Some fellow teacher you're having a fling with? No, can't be that.'

'Why not?' she immediately demanded, nettled by the look of amusement on his face. Not only had his girlfriend-in-the-wings warned her off a man she wouldn't have dreamt of having, but here was the man in question gazing at her as though trying to figure out how she could possibly ever attract anyone at all.

'Because you would have rushed back home and spilled the beans, proved your mother wrong about your marriage prospects, wouldn't you? Yes.' He answered his own question with a slow nod. 'Definitely. So if you *are* involved with someone then it can't be Mr Right. Which just leaves us with Mr Wrong. Married man, is he? Some loser cheating on his wife and two-point-two kids?'

Louis hadn't ever felt such sudden, intense curiosity. He prided himself on his ability to read people, and that included members of the opposite sex who, despite their reputation for being unfathomable, were often all too transparent as far as he was concerned.

'How dare you?' Lizzy forgot that she was ill. She forgot that her bones ached so much that even shifting under the quilt required concerted will-power. She forgot her fuzzy head, her dry mouth and her throat which felt as though it had been shredded. 'I would *never* go out with a married man!'

'Really? It's funny what people drift into, though, isn't it? Highly unsuitable relationships…' Her face was flushed and her dark hair was dramatic against the pristine white of the pillow. What was she wearing? he wondered. Was she one of those women whose underwear belied their outward appearance? Was she the leather-jacket-wearing motorbike rider who liked the feel of silk, satin and lace against her skin? Like a runaway horse, his imagination broke its rein and galloped off at furious speed. Hell; he could feel himself getting worked up at the thought of her in a sensible cotton bra and granny knickers! What the hell was wrong with him?

He was forced to turn away and look out of the window

at the falling snow with his back to her, so that she couldn't make out the evidence of his attraction bulging in his pants.

'I wouldn't be so stupid,' Lizzy hotly denied, to his back.

'No, of course not.' Louis, composed again, turned around and looked her squarely in the face. Being cooped up in this place was beginning to do crazy things to him. Women like the one lying in the bed weren't his type. He liked them taller, fuller breasted, preferably blonde and very, very compliant.

And, whilst he might indulge his women with expensive presents, he didn't like gold-diggers and the Sharp family sat firmly in that category—whatever Lizzy might have to say on the subject. And he had plenty. 'You still haven't said what you would like to eat—and, to answer your question about who would be in charge of making it, I've inherited sufficient help to ensure that the nuts and bolts of this place keep ticking over till it's completely renovated and more staff can be brought on board.'

'I didn't see anyone yesterday.'

'I'd given them the evening off and they were in their quarters.'

'Oh. Right. Well, maybe I could have something light,' she said, knowing that he wouldn't leave until she asked for something. 'Some toast and maybe an egg would be fine. Thank you.'

'And I'll bring you some more tablets, or else your sister will, although she's somewhere in the bowels of this place with Nicholas and I lack the desire to hunt them down.'

'I should, um, thank you for...' She made a vague, all-encompassing gesture. 'Also for coming to get me when my motorbike broke down.' She didn't want to press him on what exactly had happened to her motorbike, which was her responsibility after all, but he must have read her mind.

He said without waiting to be asked, 'The snow is supposed to clear by tomorrow and I've arranged for it to be collected and taken to the garage for servicing.'

'You shouldn't have,' Lizzy said politely.

'Oh, but that's where you're wrong.' Louis perched on the side of the bed and noticed the way she edged fractionally away from him. 'If you stress over that bike of yours, well, stress isn't going to set you on the road to a swift recovery, is it?'

Lizzy felt her breath catch in her throat. He was mesmerising, mesmerising in a way that made the hairs on the back of her neck stand on end, which surely couldn't be a good thing?

'And I want you back on your feet as soon as possible, because you and I need to have a bracing little chat, and it should wait until you're fit and strong.'

'A bracing little chat?' Lizzy wondered why she didn't care for the sound of that. 'Bracing little chats' were what she gave her schoolchildren when they had been particularly naughty.

'About some information that's recently come into my possession.'

'I have no idea what you're talking about.'

'I'm finding that hard to believe. Surely there are no secrets in that close-knit family of yours?'

'We're pretty open with each other.' Lizzy dragged the syllables out while she tried to work out where he was going with that enigmatic statement. On another level, her senses were wildly reacting to his proximity, drinking in the sharp, beautiful, dangerous angles of his face and the easy, graceful strength of his body.

'Then it should come as no surprise to you that your father is now heavily in debt and in desperate need of cash or else he might just find himself without a roof over his head.'

'What are you talking about?' Lizzy whispered.

She had blanched, and for an instant Louis felt a rush of guilty awareness that he might have gone too far with this revelation. But he couldn't help feeling that Rose's sudden, demonstrative affection for his friend, after what had seemed a certain amount of indifference, had its roots in something less than innocent. He had expected to see a flicker of something on Lizzy's face, something that would indicate that she knew all about her father's difficulties. Now, he could have kicked himself for not feeling out the ground before shooting his mouth off. But the words were out and couldn't be retracted.

'I don't believe you,' Lizzy eventually said in a shaky voice, and Louis shook his head to rid himself of the ridiculous feeling that he had somehow been a complete bastard. Hell, he was looking after his own! Since when had anyone ever been able to divert him from a course of action once he had set his mind to it?

'Believe it.' He stood up to put some distance between them because the scent of her was wafting through his head and threatening to derail his cool-headed self-assurance. 'Now, I'll send your food up. If you want anything else, just phone through to the kitchens. There will always be someone available.'

He was irritated with himself for dithering, but she had turned her head away, and with a click of his tongue he left the room, quietly shutting the door behind him.

CHAPTER FOUR

FOR once the weather forecasters got it right, and two days later the snow had stopped completely and in its place was a splendid, cloudless blue sky and bright, cold sun.

Dosed up on painkillers and determined to get back to her own house, Lizzy practically had to wrench herself free from Rose, who had settled into a Florence Nightingale routine that included hot drinks on demand and lengthy conversations about Nicholas: he was her big love. She had saved herself for him but she didn't regret it. He hadn't proposed as yet, but she could feel it in her bones that a proposal was just a heartbeat away, and she would say yes! But would Mum and Dad be able to afford a lavish wedding? They did have five daughters, after all... Well, provided all five got married...

Which proved conclusively that she knew nothing about their financial situation.

Which made Lizzy think that perhaps Louis had fabricated the whole sorry story to sow dissension in the ranks, even though she knew, somewhere deep inside her, that every word he had said had been true.

Not that she could corner him and get him to give her more details, because as soon as the last flake of snow had fallen, and the courtyard had been cleared, he had taken off back to London in a blur of noise and whirring helicopter-blades.

Jessica and Eloise had gone with him, no doubt desperate to return to civilisation—where they could choose between three hundred types of coffee at the snap of a finger in chintzy little cafés, and where wellies came in attractive patterns and fetching colours and weren't designed for anything more strenuous than having a lazy stroll through Kew Gardens.

'Won't this place feel way too big with just the two of you in it?' Lizzy had ventured, and then had listened to how really remarkably small it was when you just occupied a handful of rooms and ignored the rest.

With a sinking heart Lizzy knew, as soon as she walked through the front door and was ushered inside by her parents, that everything Louis had said had been one-hundred percent true: neither of them seemed in the least bit shocked or disappointed that Rose had decided to stay on with Nicholas.

'We'll be seeing them soon enough,' her mother said over dinner. 'I've just come off the phone from Nicholas, in fact. I was suggesting that it might be a nice idea to have a little Christmas party at Crossfeld. The weather's going to be fine for the next few weeks, apparently, and it would be lovely to show willing to all the folk around here. After all, he's going to be relying on them for lots of practical help once work starts on the place in the New Year. You know how it works around here,' Grace continued comfortably. 'It's always good to get in with the locals.'

'He might feel a bit uncomfortable with all the fuss and attention.' Lizzy speared a pea on her plate, thought better of it and closed her knife and fork. Next to her Maisie and Leigh were busy dissecting Nicholas's sisters and conducting a silly conversation about which rich and famous person they would most like to turn up to the Christmas party at Crossfeld—because obviously Louis was so rich that he would be sure to know hundreds of beautiful people.

'Hundreds of beautiful people might not see the wilds of Scotland in winter as the most desirable place to be,' Lizzy said irritably. 'And, anyway, where would all these beautiful people stay? Half of the house is closed off.'

She had planned to get her father to one side so that she could probe him about the so-called debt that was hanging like an albatross around his neck, according to Louis. But there was no chance of that with Maisie and Leigh dominating the conversation in their usual high-spirited manner. Her father smiled and occasionally joined in and her mother lapsed into dreamy predictions of a forthcoming marriage, which was enough to make Lizzy squirm in her chair.

'Marriage is a really big commitment,' she heard herself saying in the sort of prissy voice that had her sisters yawning and rolling their eyes to the ceiling, butting in to tell her that the only thing Rose ever wanted was to settle down and have a bundle of kids. 'You shouldn't try and rush Rose into anything!' she persevered. But it was difficult to strike the right note when both her parents were busy clearing the table and stacking the dishwasher, apparently not paying much attention to a word she was saying.

'Why can't you just be happy for your sister?' Grace asked sharply, finally picking up on Lizzy's fourth attempt to quell her mother's simmering excitement over a marriage that had yet to be proposed—and a wedding that stood a very good chance of coming to nothing. 'Instead of just sitting there and finding all the reasons why she and Nicholas shouldn't be in a relationship.'

'They're not... There are lots of differences between them. They come from two completely different worlds, Mum...'

'Not everyone thinks it's a stumbling block to fall for a wealthy man, Lizzy,' her father said, sitting down and looking at her across the table. 'Because someone has money doesn't disqualify them from the race.'

'I know *that*.'

'And besides.' He lowered his voice, but Maisie and Leigh had disappeared off to the lure of reality TV and wouldn't have heard him if he had been shouting at the top of his lungs. 'Things are a little tight here at the moment, to be honest. A few bad investments. At any rate, we've had to remortgage the house and I can't pretend that it wouldn't help if Rose married Nicholas. I might just be able to put a business proposition to him that could be a life belt for us.'

'And don't you go breathing a word of this to your sisters,' her mother warned, but her face was drawn when she pulled up a chair to sit next to her husband. 'We're telling you because you've your head screwed on. Maisie and Leigh, well, heaven only knows where *their* heads are—and thank the Lord that Vivian isn't here to lecture us on your father's bad investments! And Rose... Well, she deserves her stab at happiness.'

'So in other words you've pushed Rose together with Nicholas because he's rich and you'd like him to help you out of a hole.' She regretted it as soon as the words were out.

'Rose fell for that young man the minute she saw him,' her father said in a tone Lizzy had never heard before, then he smiled that crooked smile he always saved for her. 'She's as romantic as they come, Busy Lizzy; you of all people should know that. If your mother and I had wanted to shove any of you into marrying a man for his money, we would have looked no further than you.'

'Why is that?' She smiled weakly back at them but something inside her twisted.

'Because you're tough and hard-headed, and out of all you girls you're the one who would be able to see marriage as a business proposition. Not—' he sat back and diffused his remark with a chuckle '—that your mum and I would ever do that.'

Louis—Lizzy thought later, lying in the bedroom she had shared with Rose a million years ago when they had been children—saw her as an arrogant tough-nut with too much of a mouth on her. Would he ever have spoken to any other woman on the face of the earth the way he had spoken to her? Her parents saw her as hard-headed and practical but in a way that didn't seem particularly endearing. To Maisie and Leigh, she was too serious, the last person they would think of inviting to one of their wild parties at university. And Vivian… Well, Vivian lived in a world of her own.

And who could she blame but herself for the way the rest of the world perceived her? She had always been the one who braved the elements with her father at football games. She knew more about rugby than most of the guys she had ever dated. She rode a motorbike, which seemed a pretty practical mode of transport, as far as she was concerned, but which most people found a little strange. Was it any wonder that Louis took no trouble to spare her feelings when it came to telling her how things stood? Any wonder that the whole subject of marriage an ongoing background chant from her mother for as long as she could remember, had never actually been applied to *her*?

She sternly told herself that she was perfectly happy with things exactly the way they were. But the following morning, fully recovered and in no mood to spend the day brooding, she packed an overnight bag and announced that she was going back down to London. But she would return for the Christmas period, she added hurriedly, knowing when to change her plans in order to avoid confrontation. So that she could *go to the ball*. Like Cinderella.

'I know they're not actually expecting me at school.' She grabbed a slice of toast on the move whilst checking on her phone to see what time the cheapest train would be running. 'But I have stuff to collect. And I have to tell Colleen and Paula that I won't be sharing their alternative Christmas.'

There were also several other things she would have to do, although these she would be keeping under her hat. The first would be to buy something really special for the wretched party at Crossfeld, something sexy and pretty which hadn't been hurriedly borrowed from one of her sisters. Then she would look up Louis at his London house and, instead of attacking him and baring her teeth, she would try and plead Rose's cause—and she would also try and use a few feminine wiles when she did it.

More than ever now, it seemed vital that he understood how deeply in love Rose was with Nicholas and how important it would be if he could just give them both his blessing. Soft-spoken, bespectacled Nicholas was in awe of his sophisticated, predatory friend; would love actually conquer all if Louis got it into his head to break up the relationship? Lizzy had her doubts.

But, more than ever, Louis would think that he had the right to protect his friend. The Sharp family was in trouble finan-cially and with everything to win; he would find it perfectly understandable that Rose would be chosen as the sacrificial lamb: beautiful, shy Rose. He would see that as the essence of a good gold-digger. He lived and breathed cynicism. If he had reluctantly been coming round to giving them the benefit of the doubt, that would have been blown out of the sky by revelations of her father's financial situation.

When Lizzy thought about it, she had to grit her teeth together and remind herself that trying to bludgeon her way through to him wasn't going to work. For Louis Jumeau, women should be creatures of grace and beauty, and if they weren't he had no time for them.

On the train down, she managed to get his address from Rose with a series of half lies and half truths. She *did* want to see him but he certainly *hadn't* made any promises about donating money to the school. And it *was* vital that she saw him straight away rather than wait, though not because the school was about to close and she wanted to sort things out before everyone disappeared for the Christmas break. She even managed to get his mobile number, which apparently was only given to a few select people. Lizzy heard this and had to suppress a snort of laughter. Who did the man think he was?

And wouldn't it be funny if he was besieged with thousands of unwanted calls because she had sold his number online?

The following day, however, there was nothing amusing about her situation. She had arranged to meet Louis that evening for dinner at a restaurant in Belgravia and she suspected that the only reason he had agreed had been out of curiosity. He would be wondering what she could possibly have of interest to say to him. Hadn't he already laid down the ground rules? What else could there be to say on the subject?

She had dashed from school to the shops and had bought herself an outfit so out of her comfort zone that she was almost scared to remove it from its tissue paper and put it on in the privacy of her bedroom.

But put it on she did. The red-and-white-checked mini-skirt hugged her and showed off legs that were slender and well shaped. The long-sleeved, body-hugging ribbed jumper, also in a startling shade of red, was modest yet managed to suggest curves she hadn't really known she possessed. And she now owned a pair of very high ankle boots—which, she grudgingly admitted, looked passable.

There was nothing she could do about her coat or her bag but the small, *faux* fur hat was stylish.

She made sure to arrive late. Not so late that there was a risk that he may just become bored and leave, but late enough to ensure that he would be already there when she arrived.

And he was, sitting in a corner of the discreet, very posh French restaurant. It was a prime seat for looking at who was entering the restaurant, but Louis had the *Financial Times* in front of him and was nursing a drink. Lizzy took a deep breath and steadied her fraying nerves. It would have been easy to give in to that fleeting moment of panic, but instead she gathered herself and walked confidently towards him. She could feel heads turning to look at her, and for the first time she understood why Maisie and Leigh—and even Rose, to some extent—were so obsessed with clothes. In her small skirt, tight top and high shoes, and with her hair tumbling down her back, she felt sexy.

When she was standing in front of Louis and he finally looked up, she felt a surge of pleasure because, controlled as he was, he couldn't conceal that flash of pure, sexual appreciation.

'Sorry I'm a bit late,' she said carelessly. 'Traffic.'

'As in you stopping it?'

Lizzy blushed furiously and sat down.

'Nice outfit,' he drawled, once again composed.

'Oh, it's just some old thing I grabbed from the back of the wardrobe.' The wine being poured in her glass was a blessed distraction, as was the over-sized menu when it arrived. Her nerves began to settle over the polite pleasantries about her health and the weather and the small amount of information she volunteered about the school Christmas play she was helping to produce.

She was acutely aware of his legs under the table and the fact that they were only centimetres away from her own. As he leaned forward to signal the waiter to take their order, his knee actually brushed against hers and she had to restrain herself from giving a little startled yelp.

'So...' Louis sat back in his chair, tilting his body so that he could stretch out his long legs. 'Now that we've politely done the pleasantries, are you going to tell me why you're here? Or did you just decide that you wanted me to see your sexy side?'

Dark eyes roved lazily over her body, taking in the high breasts—fuller than he would have expected in someone so slender—her thin, graceful hands and her stubborn, strong, intelligent face—which wasn't classically beautiful but was arresting, he was finally forced to acknowledge. She had the sort of face that he felt compelled to stare at, and that irritated and amused him at the same time.

'If you want me to remark on it, then I'm more than happy to oblige. You're sexy. I like the way that top fits you. You really do yourself a disservice by dressing like a guy. And you should never tie your hair back, it looks good like that. Is it as soft as it looks?' He leaned forward and twirled some strands around his fingers; for one heart-stopping moment everything inside her was thrown into frantic disarray. God, was she *attracted* to this man? Surely not? Yet her body was suddenly hot and heavy and she could feel her chest lift with every breath, her blood pounding through her veins.

'That's not why I'm here.' She pointedly gathered her hair with one hand and draped it behind her. 'I haven't dressed like this to prove anything.' *Hadn't she?* 'I don't want you to find me sexy. I think we've already concluded that we just aren't each other's cup of tea. I would have been more than happy to come here in jeans and a jumper but I figured that this restaurant might have a dress code.' He was looking at her with such unblinking, shuttered intensity that it was making her as nervous as a kitten. 'And please stop staring at me like that!'

'When you dress like that, you should be prepared to be stared at.'

'I came to have a conversation about Rose. Okay, well, about Rose and Nicholas.' Food arrived and she sat back to allow the waiter to produce her main course of *poussin* with an elaborate flourish. 'I… What you said about Dad being in a bit of financial bother is, well, true.' She snaked a tongue nervously over dry lips, and when she glanced across at him his expression was closed and uninviting. 'I think he's invested badly and he said something about having to remortgage the house. So I can understand what's going on in your head.'

Louis maintained a steady silence. Had she known him at all, she would have known that begging missions never worked. He took a sip of wine and began eating, waiting for her to carry on.

'You were cynical to start with and I guess that you're even more cynical now that you've poked around in my father's life and unearthed his financial situation. I suppose you're really proud of having done that.'

'I think we're beginning to go over old territory here, Lizzy. And doing a background check on someone isn't unusual. It's always a good idea to have the full picture.'

'You don't *want* the full picture. You just see what you want to see!' She made an inarticulate sound under her breath and flung her hands up in frustration.

Frankly, that should have been the cue for Louis to bring the meal to an abrupt but necessary end. Outbursts in public places, while he could not care less what people thought of him, weren't his style.

But her cheeks were flushed and she had shoved the sleeves of her tight jumper up, exposing slim, firm hands. She didn't seem to have noticed, but in the heat of the moment not only had her hair swung forward, tempting him to take some of the silky strands between his fingers yet again, but her knees were brushing his—and that was doing some interesting things to his body.

'Rose doesn't know anything about, well, about *anything*.'

'Maybe we're getting a little over-excited here about nothing. How was the food? You don't seem to be eating.'

'The food's great.' She took a mouthful. It really was great—just a shame that she wasn't in the mood to appreciate it. 'And what do you mean about getting over-excited about nothing?'

'I mean you seem to be under the illusion that Rose and Nicholas are destined for the altar.'

'Illusion? Has Nicholas told you that he's going to dump my sister?'

'Nicholas hasn't confided in me one way or another, but let's face facts. He got sent up to Scotland to handle some of

the ground work on Crossfeld. Nicholas's family might have
their pile in the country, but he's only ever been accustomed
to life in London.' Louis shrugged, a man-of-the-world shrug,
as though every word he was saying and every assumption he
was making was shot through with unarguable fact. 'Scotland
would have been like another planet. It's natural that he would
have gravitated towards the first sympathetic attractive woman
he met.'

'You're saying that Rose is just someone to keep him company until he can get back to his normal life?'

'I'm saying that it might be a mistake for your sister to start
thinking about wedding bells—and even more of a mistake
for your parents to start imagining that a rich son-in-law might
bail them out of their financial difficulties.'

Lizzy thought she could detect an edge of contempt in
his voice and her hackles rose. He might very well sit there,
watching her with those lazy, dark, fabulous eyes, sneering at
the little Scottish upstart of a woman who fancied her chances
with a guy whose family owned a *pile in the country*—but
when had he ever had to worry about money? 'They're not
imagining anything of the sort.' She defended her family
stoutly, and Louis raised his eyebrows in polite disbelief.

Fetching though she might look, she wasn't fetching enough
to override the glaring evidence in front of him. Firstly, the
coincidence of Nicholas falling for the beautiful damsel with
the impoverished background, although it had only become
clear *just* how impoverished the background was. Secondly,
the fact that Rose, from everything he had witnessed, had
hardly behaved like a woman in love until, mysteriously, she
had decided to mount a more concentrated campaign—which
naturally included engineering her way into Crossfeld and
climbing into bed with Nicholas. Had her parents become a
little more active in their encouragement of the relationship?
Grace Sharp had certainly not been reticent in showing her
delight at the match.

Granted, Lizzy might have been out of the loop in terms of the nuts and bolts of what had been going on, but was that his problem?

'You don't believe in love, do you?' she asked sourly, and Louis laughed and raked his fingers through his hair.

'I believe in lust and I believe in the institution of marriage.'

'You mean marriage based on…what? How can you base a marriage on lust? Lust doesn't last.'

Louis relaxed and ordered coffee. This, he discovered, was more like the conversation with her that he had had in mind. 'But it's an enjoyable starting point, don't you agree? Not that I've given much thought to marriage one way or the other.'

Lizzy shifted awkwardly. She realised that her legs were brushing against his and she primly angled her body away from his—except, when their eyes met, she could see at a glance that he had noted the shift and was amused by it. 'And what happens when the lust fades away?'

'Oh, that's why it's so important to be practical when it comes to getting married. A decent business arrangement doesn't allow for any nasty surprises. There's no such thing as the perfect marriage, but there *is* such a thing as the perfect criteria for a wife, and it involves lack of hassle and no ugly suspicions of an ulterior motive. And, do me a favour, don't get onto your soap box and start preaching to me about class differences and how we rich people have the wrong priorities.'

The perfect criteria. A shard of pain stabbed her as she remembered Jessica's warning about reading signs behind his bored, idle flirting, if that was what it had been. When it came to the *perfect criteria*, she was nowhere on the scale. Not that it even mattered! And yet…

'I wasn't about to say anything of the sort. *That* would just be stating the obvious. Actually, I was going to tell you that there's a guy talking to the head waiter by the front door and I think he's looking for you…'

'Oh, good God,' Louis muttered darkly under his breath and Lizzy looked at him incredulously.

'You look a little uncomfortable, Louis. Are you trying to *hide*? It won't wash. I think he's spotted you.'

'Of course I wasn't trying to hide. Don't be ridiculous.' He glared at her and then stiffened as the young blond man approached their table and greeted him from behind.

'Louis! Have you any idea how long it took me to find you?' He sat down at the table and turned the full wattage of his smile on Lizzy. 'Of course, if I'd known that you were on a hot date with a *very* sexy lady I might not have come down. I'm Freddy Dale, by the way.'

He held out his hand and Lizzy was charmed by the smile that hit her like a ray of sunshine. At a guess, he couldn't have been more than twenty-five, but it was difficult to tell with his boyish, blond good looks and the bright-blue eyes that sparkled playfully. Next to him Louis, frowning and terse, and as dark as Freddy was fair, bristled with disapproval—which had the perverse effect of stimulating her interest. She inclined her body towards Freddy, resting her elbow on the table and cupping her chin with the palm of her hand.

'And I'm Lizzy.'

'As you can tell, I'm busy, Freddy. Was there something you wanted?'

'It can wait. I'm much more eager to find out all about this delicious creature sitting here with you.' He included Lizzy in a conspiratorial grin. 'At the risk of sounding impertinent, you're not exactly Louis's type.'

'I know.' Lizzy couldn't fail but smile back. 'We've already established that.'

'He goes for blondes.'

'Freddy, I'm not in the mood, so get to the point and leave.'

Lizzy heard the authority in Louis's voice, the hint of steel that offered her a glimpse of the man who should never be crossed. On hearing it, too, Freddy's smile dropped and he turned to Louis with a truculent, languid expression.

'I thought I might have a bit of an advance on my salary.'

'You *work* for Louis?' Lizzy couldn't believe it because he was just the sort of guy she could not imagine Louis employing. Not that she had any real idea what the quality of his employees was like, but she imagined them as a cowering bunch, keen to salute at the crack of the whip.

'And why do you need an advance on your salary?' Louis made no pretence of hiding his impatience.

Freddy flushed and slanted an uncomfortable look at Lizzy. 'I'd really rather not discuss this in front of your delightful date.'

'I'm not his date.'

'No?' This time, it was Freddy's turn to be curious, but Louis was having none of it. He looked pointedly at his watch; regrettably—because he had actually been enjoying his sparring companion—decided that dinner would have to come to an end.

'No,' Lizzy began, already sympathising with the poor man who was now finding himself subjected to the full force of Louis's powerful personality. 'Actually…'

Louis held up one imperious hand and her voice trailed off.

'I really don't give a damn about what you would or would not rather do, Freddy. Just say what you came here to say and clear off.'

'Okay. May I?' He helped himself to a glass of what wine was left and nodded approvingly at the bottle. 'Do you remember that girl I was dating?'

'No.'

'Perhaps I should leave,' Lizzy muttered, embarrassed, but Louis waved her back into her seat without looking at her. Because even a gesture as slight as that seemed to allow no room for disobedience, she sat back down and tried to appear insouciant as she sipped some of her coffee.

'Eleanor King. I think you met her a couple of times,' Freddy muttered awkwardly, talking to a profile, because Louis had inclined his head to one side and appeared to be indifferent to what was being said to him as he idly surveyed his surroundings.

Lizzy had absolutely no doubt that he was taking everything in and would probably have been able to repeat the entire conversation word for word if asked.

'You mean the plain, overweight young girl who happened to be the heir to a massive fortune?'

Freddy's face darkened but he was still trying to smile through his obvious resentment. 'I'm no longer involved with her, but unfortunately I may have gone over my head when it came to spending on her. Jewellery. A couple of expensive weekends abroad; that sort of thing.'

'And what does this have to do with me and advancing your salary?'

'Look, I know I should live within my means—and, believe me, this won't happen again. Do you think I *enjoy* being here, asking you to lend me money?'

Louis sighed elaborately and rubbed his eyes with his thumbs. 'Possibly rather more than I enjoy having you here with your hand outstretched. Again. If it weren't for the fact that I have an obligation to you, Freddy, I would have you chucked onto the street without a moment's hesitation.'

Lizzy sneaked a sympathetic glance over to Freddy, who clearly knew when to keep his mouth shut and duck low. But after a few minutes a cheque was made out for the money he was after and shoved across the table. Which instantly restored Freddy's good mood, although he was standing up now, eager to leave, as charming as ever as he made his departure, leaning to bring Lizzy's hand to his lips and to tell her that he would be seeing her very soon.

'Jessica, Nicholas's sister, has invited me to a do her brother's having at Crossfeld,' he said, tucking the cheque carefully into his wallet. 'And I can't wait. Make a change from London.'

Louis inserted with deadly accuracy, 'As opposed to Barbados, where you spent *last* Christmas, if I remember correctly?'

They both watched Freddy disappear out of the restaurant and then Lizzy turned to Louis and said lightly, 'He seemed nice.'

Louis sat back and looked at her unsmilingly. 'And you base that on *what*, exactly?'

'Well, he's very cheerful, and I gather from the conversation that he's not too clued up when it comes to money.'

'As understatements go, that one's right up there.'

'But, then, neither am I, as a matter of fact. I can never resist spending whatever I have as soon as the rent's paid. By the time the end of the month rolls round, I'm usually too broke to do anything but stay inside and watch television.'

'You should abort this conversation before it goes any further. And, as far as Freddy goes, you know nothing about the situation, so maybe you should bear that in mind when you're forming your judgements.'

'At least he laughs now and again. At least he's light-hearted and fun!'

'I could show you a lot of fun.'

And just like that the atmosphere altered, shifted into some weird gear that Lizzy couldn't get to grips with. She opened her mouth to return with something clever and cutting but nothing emerged. She watched as he very, very slowly smiled at her, a lazy, knowing smile that made her toes curl and the hairs on the back of her neck stand on end.

'I should, um, go. It's late and I just came to, well, try and plead with you to give Rose the benefit of the doubt.' She stood up clumsily and distracted herself from those piercing black eyes by fumbling with her bag.

'Message received,' Louis said drily, signalling for the bill.

Received, Lizzy thought, addled, *but neither understood nor accepted.* But she wouldn't press further. For some reason, all she wanted to do was leave the restaurant and get back to her flat as fast as her feet would take her.

CHAPTER FIVE

LIZZY would have enjoyed the Christmas celebrations a lot more if she hadn't been wracked with anxiety on so many fronts that trying to simply focus on one was nigh on impossible.

There was the problem of Rose, who had returned from Crossfeld convinced for some reason that the party which Nicholas summarily had been volunteered to throw—on the flimsy grounds that he needed to make his mark with the local community who had welcomed him with open arms—was going to be the occasion for their engagement to be announced. Lizzy did her utmost to bring her back down to earth, but, like a balloon filled with helium, the second her restraining hand was removed up it floated once again.

Then there was the nagging worry about her parents' finances. How could they possibly have afforded the presents? The massive Christmas tree groaning with decorations? The extravagant Christmas day lunch? They didn't seem to have curtailed their expenses at all. On the one occasion when Lizzy tried to tactfully mention 'the money subject', she was met with vague murmurings that everything would be all right. By which she assumed that they really were banking on Rose marrying Nicholas and his fabulous bank balance.

Which made her instantly think of Louis with his contemptuous, lazy eyes—and the second she began thinking of

Louis her mind wouldn't stop. Image upon image crowded in until her head hurt.

On top of which, Maisie and Leigh's endless speculative chatter about the upcoming party was driving her crazy.

Although there was a part of her that was also stupidly looking forward to that date in the calendar: the day after Boxing Day. Anyone would think that she had never been to a party before. But in bed at night, with the lights off and the constant chatter silent, she found that she was picturing herself in her newly purchased dress, which she had yet to reveal to any of her sisters.

She had bought it the day before she had left London to return to Scotland, and as with the flamboyant mini, it was something she would previously have bypassed without a second glance, never thinking that anything colourful could ever possibly suit her.

When had she started the process of pigeon-holing herself? she wondered. When had she taken up the mantel of the serious-minded daughter who had no time for the pointless frivolities of her sisters? Of course, Vivian, who was staying on in Africa over Christmas—and had piously instructed everyone to donate any money they might have spent on her Christmas presents to the orphanage where she was currently working—held the position of the virtuous member of the family. But Lizzy had gradually become the sharp, opinionated daughter. And over time she had dressed the part. Teaching didn't require a smart, fancy suit and her wardrobe had dwindled to a selection of suitable clothes: jeans, leggings, and baggy jumpers of indeterminate colour that could withstand playground duty and art classes with eight-year-old kids.

But, when she had walked into that restaurant and seen the flash of appreciation in Louis's eyes, something inside her had stirred.

So the day after Boxing Day, with Christmas out of the

way and her siblings busily getting themselves prepared for the party, Lizzy surreptitiously fetched her finery out of the bowels of the wardrobe and spread it out on her bed for inspection.

It was long-sleeved, figure hugging, and hundreds of sequins in varying shades of blue glittered whenever she moved. It was a statement dress from someone who had grown accustomed to scorning statement dresses.

And when she made her appearance, the very last of the Sharp household to descend the staircase, it was to five upturned, open-mouthed, speechless faces.

Not only was she wearing a sequined dress, but she was also wearing very high, iridescent blue shoes—and instead of her usual black coat, she had a very deep blue cape draped over her shoulders.

Of course, the speechlessness was short lived, then Maisie and Leigh were swarming around her, trying to unearth the label of the dress while Rose winked and gave her the thumbs-up sign. Her mother contented herself with declaring for anyone interested that at long last all her advice about dressing to impress had paid off, because no child of hers should have ever contemplated a never-ending diet of jeans and leather jackets.

The only crazy thought in her head whilst all this was going on around her was what was Louis going to think? Then she had to sternly remind herself that she didn't care what he thought. Whether he knew it or not, he was the property of the very suitable Jessica, or someone like her who fitted *the perfect criteria;* they were poles apart and could have evolved from different planets. His snobbishness enraged her and contradicted every principle she had ever held dear.

None of it helped very much when, half an hour later, they pulled up into the courtyard. It had been decorated with the sort of style only vast sums of money could buy, and there was valet parking, so that they were relieved of their people carrier as soon as it drew up to the front door.

The house itself was ablaze with lights. They must have given some of the rooms in the wing that had been closed off a bit of an airing, because surely there would be numerous people staying over? She didn't know about Nicholas, but she suspected that Louis's pulling power and influence was so far reaching that at the snap of his finger he would easily have been able to command a full house, even in Scotland in the depths of winter.

Although it had to be said that the weather was behaving particularly kindly at the moment—bitterly cold, but blue skies had driven back the relentless rain and snow that always threatened any event at this time of year.

They entered the house, which was packed with people, some familiar but most not. Waiters were scurrying through the crowds, holding their trays high, and through one of the doors drifted the sound of very mellow jazz music.

In true festive spirit, the decorations were elaborate and seasonal, and had obviously been done by professionals working with a bottomless financial fund.

Immediately upon entering, Rose excused herself so that she could locate Nicholas, and Maisie and Leigh disappeared into the throng, buoyant and excited at the prospect of spotting some celebrities.

'You're going to mingle, aren't you, pet?' her father asked as he spotted a golf buddy across the room.

Lizzy gulped. She had been relieved of her coat by one of the army of helpers employed for the event, and now felt as conspicuous as an elephant in a china shop. But mingle she would, especially as her parents were on the point of deserting her. They had recognised friends and—her mother being her mother—she, like Maisie and Leigh, would be avid with curiosity about the hordes of people there, some of whom, she muttered, she already recognised from the telly.

'I'd wager there are *lots* of eligible bachelors here, Lizzy,' she muttered with a glint in her eye, which was Lizzy's cue to propel herself through the crowds, stopping en route to grab a glass of champagne from a passing waiter.

The house was extensive and the rooms on the ground floor were all opened up. In several of them, buffets had been laid out for anyone who wanted to help themselves. In the massive lounging area, she discovered the source of the jazz music, a live quartet. Because this room was less noisy and less demanding than every other room she had entered, she edged towards one of the free tables and allowed herself to keep time with the music, tapping her feet lightly, and smiling because she recognised the tune.

She looked stunning, Louis thought, sipping his drink and lounging against the door. He wondered whether he had been looking out for her or whether he had just happened to notice her the second she had walked through the front door. He also wondered how it was that, although she was classically less beautiful than her sisters—in fact classically less beautiful than a lot of the women there, many of whom made it their business to look beautiful—she still managed to drag his attention like no one else.

He also wondered whether she was the reason he had gone all out to ensure that this party, which technically wasn't even his, was as elaborate and impressive as it undoubtedly was. He wasn't the kind of guy who liked parties to start with, and would certainly never have instigated an extravaganza on this scale, least of all because there had been no need for his involvement in the first place.

But he had overridden Nicholas's far more modest suggestions and taken time out to implement his own.

For her—to impress her like a kid with a teenage crush? Louis squashed that unsettling thought before it had time to take root. But, hell, she had been on his mind too much, resurfacing with annoying ease even when he attempted to apply reason by telling himself that she was little more than a nuisance.

And now… His eyes lingered on the way the dress clung to her body, before he pushed himself away from the door and headed in her direction.

Over the sound of the saxophone, she was unaware of his approach until she felt his breath warm against her neck, and heard his lazy drawl as he asked her whether she was having a good time.

Lizzy started, spilling some of her champagne, and turned around. She hadn't seen him, although her stomach had churned at the knowledge that he was in the house somewhere.

'Thank you. Yes.' She took a step back because his proximity was wrapping itself around her and stifling her ability to think clearly. 'It's very…er…fancy. Lots of people.' He looked drop-dead gorgeous in a pair of dark trousers, a white shirt which he had cuffed to the elbows and a bow tie with a swirly paisley pattern, which she found herself staring at because looking directly at him made her jittery. Very quickly, she swallowed the remainder of her champagne. 'Are these all friends of Nicholas?' she carried on.

'Mutual friends.' Louis gave an indifferent shrug.

'How on earth did they all get here?'

'Let me put it this way, they had lots of fun taking over the first-class carriages on the trains up. The rest flew.'

'I'm surprised they made the effort.'

'Are you? I invited them.'

'And naturally they wouldn't consider refusing.'

'You got it in one.' *Since when had he been prone to uttering statements of that nature?* 'Dance with me,' he said abruptly and Lizzy's eyes widened in surprise.

'Dance with you? Why?'

'Do I have to provide a reason?' Louis asked irritably. 'I'm being polite. After our acrimonious dinner the other evening,

I think it might be a good idea to call a truce, at least for the duration of this party.' Had he ever been turned down by a woman for a dance? Louis didn't think so.

'Is...is Freddy here?' Lizzy asked, shying away from the thought of being held by Louis to the very slow number being played.

Instantly Louis stiffened and narrowed his eyes on her. 'Why do you ask?'

'I just wondered. He said that he was going to come.'

'And is that the reason you've dressed to kill? Forget it. No money there.'

'I knew it! You just can't be polite to me for more than five seconds, can you?' In a curious way, it felt good to be angry with him because it camouflaged far more disturbing responses. 'So, in answer to your question, no—I *don't* want to dance with you!' But she wasn't quick enough to dart away and she felt his hand circle her wrist. It was like having a live current shot through her. She almost gasped aloud, and when she spoke her voice was thin and uneven.

'What do you think you're doing...?'

'I apologise. I shouldn't have said that.'

'I still won't dance with you,' Lizzy muttered. She clung frantically to the thought that he was still tarring her with the same prejudiced brush that he had used to tar her entire family.

'Why? Are you scared?'

'Scared of what? I'm not scared of anything.'

'Because I don't bite,' he said softly. And then with amusement is his voice, 'At least, not until I'm asked.' He held out his hand and, after having announced her lack of fear of anything, Lizzy had no option but to allow herself to be led to the small area that had been cleared for dancing.

The slow music played on. His arm went round her waist and the feel of his muscular body against hers brought a soft groan to her lips. This wasn't right, she thought feverishly.

This was dancing with the enemy. But without even thinking her head rested against his shoulder and her body, wilful and disobedient, moulded against his as she let him guide her.

She didn't know whether he was even aware of it, but his thumb was making small, erotic circles against her back and she shivered and drew fractionally closer to him.

Thank the good Lord the music didn't allow for conversation, because her tongue had clamped tight to the roof of her mouth.

It took a few seconds to surface after the song had drawn to its mellow conclusion, and she made a show of instantly pulling back and rearranging her dress.

'There. See? I've danced with you.'

'And did you enjoy the experience?' Louis enquired huskily. Leading question but, whatever she said to the contrary, he knew that she had enjoyed it as much as he had. Hell, he might even have enjoyed it a little too much, if that was possible.

'I like the song. It was one of my father's favourites. We all grew up with it being played non-stop in the house. I should go and look for Rose.'

'Why? She's a big girl. She can look after herself. I thought we'd established that already.'

'Yes, well…' But her feet refused to walk away, and when they finally got into gear it was to follow him out of the room and away from the crowds until they were out in what could be loosely termed the conservatory. It was more akin to an indoor courtyard, in fact, with massive urns from which spilled plants of every variety and a scattering of comfortable chairs, sofas and tables. It was easy to envisage how sumptuous it would be once it was fully renovated and the paintwork and windows repaired.

Lizzy wondered how she had arrived there. Now they were on their own and somehow a drink had found its way to her hand. She was keeping her distance, hovering by the door while he lounged indolently against the bay window, one hand shoved into his trouser pocket. But even with the distance between them she could still feel her skin tingling in response to his presence.

'Nicholas asked me something rather peculiar yesterday,' Louis said conversationally.

'What?'

'There's no need to look so wary. He asked me if I had decided to make a donation to your school.'

'Oh.' Lizzy cast him a sheepish look. 'I had to find an excuse to get your address and telephone number.'

'Very creative.'

'Not that my school doesn't need donations. There's always something that needs updating, and we don't have nearly as many computers as we'd like. Private schools have very healthy funds but state schools, well, it's a completely different story. Some of the classrooms haven't been painted in, well, years.' Lizzy knew that she was babbling while he stood there half-smiling, silent, sipping his wine and just looking at her with his head slightly tilted to one side.

'So…maybe I *will* make a donation.'

'You will?'

'Stop hovering by the door as though you're about to take flight, Lizzy.'

Lizzy supposed she could do that, considering he was thinking about donating money to her school. Really, they were having a *business* conversation, and as such there was no need to get wound up and tense. She fought back the temptation to take a deep breath and walked towards him, feeling his eyes on her as she closed the gap between them.

'You don't have to feel obliged to do that because Nicholas is under the impression that you were thinking about it.' Her voice emerged a little breathless.

'I never feel obliged to do anything because of other people

and what they might think of me. I have a considerable amount
of money set aside for charity work and donations.'

'You do?'

'I know. Difficult to think that there might be a chink in
the stereotyped image you have of me, isn't it?'

'I guess that would be company money, tax deductible
stuff…'

'All from my own private income.' He waited for that to
settle in. The mellow light shed from the two imposing lamps
in the corners of the room softened the contours of her face,
and her huge eyes were like dark wells, fringed with lashes he
knew most women would have killed for, had she but known
it. But even in a dress that would make most men stop in
their tracks and swing around for a second look she was still
ingenuously innocent of her own sexuality. She had no idea
what a turn-on that was for him. He didn't think that it was
possible for a woman to be so ludicrously removed from his
idea of femininity and yet so wildly appealing. But it seemed
that she was.

'Of course, I would have to visit the school. Inspect it. See
where my money would be allocated.'

Lizzy couldn't help it; she burst out laughing and Louis
frowned at her.

'Care to share the joke?' he said icily, which made her
laugh even harder until tears gathered in the corners of her
eyes and her jaw ached.

'No, I won't,' she said, still catching her breath. 'Somehow
I don't think you would find it very funny.' She grinned at
him and he felt his lips twitch in response.

'Try me.'

'Okay. Well, I was just trying to picture you at our school,
having a look around in your flash suit and hand-made shoes.
You wouldn't match the decor, put it that way.'

'I'm capable of dressing down.' He had to reluctantly admit
that the image was pretty amusing, even though he wasn't

ever accustomed to having the finger of fun pointed in his direction.

'Designer shirt and designer loafers?' Lizzy hazarded a guess. It felt dangerous and exhilarating to tease him. She had moved on from champagne to wine and she now polished off the rest of her glass and felt a little giddy, although the giddiness might have had something to do with the way he was looking at her.

'I could run to an old rugby shirt and trainers if you'd prefer.'

'No. You still wouldn't match the decor. You're too...'

'Too...?' Louis prompted, enjoying himself. 'Too what? Too tall? Too dark-haired? Too rich, even in the dressed-down gear?'

'Too good-looking!'

Those three words were like a shot of adrenaline. Suddenly sexual hunger sunk its teeth into him, ripping through his polished composure and making a nonsense of it. He was gripping the stem of his glass too tightly, threatening to shatter it. He carefully rested it on the wide ledge of the bay window and folded his arms.

'You find me attractive?'

'That's not what I said!'

'No?'

'I mean, of course you're an attractive man. You must know that.'

'Don't look so uncomfortable. There's nothing wrong in admitting that you're attracted to me. It's mutual, in case you're interested.'

Lizzy's mind was a whirl. How had this conversation come round? How had they gone from discussing donations to the school to the laws of sexual attraction? Had he just told her what she thought he had?

One look at his face confirmed that. His body language was relaxed and at ease but his eyes blazed with desire, and she painfully admitted to herself that what she saw there was only a reflection of what she felt herself.

A soft sound escaped her lips. She wanted to tell him that they should return to the party, that they would be missed— or at least *he* would. She doubted any member of her family would be busy hunting *her* down. Instead, what she said was, 'Sorry, but what did you just say?'

Louis smiled. His smile knocked her for six, and her head was still spinning as he lazily reached out and gave her a gentle tug, pulling her towards him.

His mouth as it hit hers had the effect of an open flame striking dry tinder. Without thinking, Lizzy stretched up, curling her arms around his neck, and lost herself in his kiss, which was hot and hard and urgent—in fact everything she had always secretly imagined a kiss should be but for her never had been.

His hand caressed her neck, tracing the delicate outline of her shoulder blades and tantalisingly playing with the neckline of her dress, a repeated seductive motion that made her want to groan out loud.

He pulled her back towards the darker reaches of the room, out of sight of anyone who might be walking past—although the conservatory was not in the main stream of traffic, and frankly where the food and alcohol lay the guests would be found. Which, thanks to the size of the house, was a distance away.

'You're beautiful,' he whispered hoarsely, slipping his finger underneath the stretchy neckline and skimming it along the top of her breast. The sequinned lycra was thick and she wasn't wearing a bra. The thought of that wreaked further havoc on his self-control.

For once, Lizzy had no desire to squash that compliment with a sarcastic rejoinder, even if the compliment probably had only arisen in the heat of the moment. She wanted to savour it and then store it away somewhere so that she could pull it out at a later date and savour it all over again.

She felt his hand caress her breast and gave a little squeal of pleasure.

'We shouldn't be doing this!' she managed to gasp.

'Reason being…?'

'Reason being that we… We don't even like each other.'

'But we want each other.'

Lizzy pulled away as his hand found the soft swell of her breast. She was shaking like a leaf. A moment of madness! The cool air barely made an impression on her heated skin and she had to step away, arms folded protectively around her.

Want and like: two small words with a telling world of difference between them. For Louis, he didn't have to like her to fancy her, and he didn't have to like her to make love to her. Emotionally and intellectually, she was so unimportant to him that he could compartmentalise her away into a one-night stand.

And she had encouraged him. One touch and she had thrown herself at him faster than a jack-in-the-box.

Where was her pride? Shame and mortification gripped her.

'What's wrong?' Louis raked his fingers through his hair and stared at her with brooding intensity.

'Nothing.' Two steps back and self-control was gathering pace, or at least she didn't feel as though she had been put through the washer. 'Neither of us should have…done what we did.'

'We didn't do anything!' Louis grated. 'Not nearly as much as both of us wanted to, and there's no point denying it.'

Lizzy preferred to skirt round that and just focus on getting away from his stifling, suffocating presence. 'I'm going to get back to the party now,' she said in an even voice. 'It would be rude of both of us not to put in an appearance at Nicholas's party. He's gone to all this trouble and I can't imagine… Well, let's just say we made a horrible mistake.'

Louis could hardly believe what he was hearing. Was this some sort of ploy—the tried and tested play-hard-to-get routine? But she was backing towards the door with determination and an expression of such mortified horror on her face that he couldn't equate her response with any kind of ploy.

But she had *wanted* him. He had felt her quiver in his arms and when she had reached up to kiss him her mouth had been as hungry and as eager as his.

He shrugged and continued watching her. 'If you want to call it a mistake, then that's fine by me, but it's just a matter of vocabulary.' He took a step towards her and she immediately took two steps back. 'The mistake happened and we both know that we want the mistake to happen again.'

'Never in a million years.'

'Don't you know that you should never lay down a gauntlet like that?'

He gave her a crooked smile and with a sick, swooning feeling Lizzy turned on her heels and fled—literally. Until she reached the safe haven of the vast drawing-room with its noise, crowds and laughter and, thank Heavens, the familiarity of her sisters. Never had she been more delighted to see Maisie and Leigh, who had managed to gather a coterie of men around them.

She was even more delighted to spot Freddy, having been served with food by one of the eight waitresses manning three long tables literally groaning with delicacies. After her shattering encounter with Louis, his unthreatening, smiling face as he made a spot on the table next to him for her to sit was like a soothing balm which she instantly wanted to apply in the hope that it might alleviate her shredded nerves.

Going anywhere near her parents or Rose would definitely be a bad move. They would spot her frazzled appearance, and

certainly neither her mother nor her sister would rest until
they had unearthed the cause of it.

But Freddy… She felt herself relaxing as she dug into her
food and listened to him gossip about the people he knew who
were at the party. People were drifting in groups towards the
tables with their plates of food. Some had vanished out to other
rooms. There was more than enough seating to accommodate
everyone. Lizzy made herself focus entirely on Freddy, just in
case her eyes started scouring the room of their own accord,
hunting out Louis. She didn't want to give in to the craven
temptation.

'Of course, all these people are here because of Louis,'
Freddy said bitterly. 'Nicholas might have a lot of friends, and
he might come from money, but Louis puts him in the shade.
He's the real mover and shaker, and if he says jump people
just nod and ask how high? He wanted to showcase his latest
pet project, so he clicked his fingers and, hey presto! Here is
his audience, ready to give him feedback if he asks.'

'You don't like him much, do you?'

'Do you?'

'Is it because you don't like your job in his company?'

Freddy's mouth curled with derision. 'I pretend to sit and
do computer work. It's not a job; it's Louis's way of paying
for a clear conscience.' He leaned towards her and she felt his
blond hair practically brush her forehead. They were huddled
together in an imitation of intimacy, and although her mind
was still tangled over thinking about Louis, it felt good to be
doing something as harmless as gossiping; if he wanted to
gossip about Louis, then that felt good, too.

She decided that she wanted to hear about Freddy's father. It
seemed he had slaved for Louis's father as his right-hand man,
taking care of the vast mansion in which Louis had grown up.
He had been promised before he died that his only son would
have the cottage in which he had lived, and sufficient money
to get off the ground, but none of that, seemingly, had come to

anything when the old man had died. Louis had immediately handed the cottage over to his chauffeur and by way of money to Freddy had instead chucked him a dead-end job in one of his companies: no chance of promotion, no chance of utilising the media studies degree he had taken; barely sufficient money to make rent on a one-room flat in Bethnal Green.

With Louis, it was all about the money. She hadn't been wrong about him! After four glasses of wine, Lizzy felt the warm glow of vindication.

She sneaked a glance around the room, which had thinned out as people had taken their food to other parts of the house, probably to the music room so that they could listen to the band as they ate. Through the open doors, the soulful strain of the jazz music was melodious and evocative.

Half-listening to Freddy on his soap box complaining about the injustice of the lot that had been dealt to him, Lizzy saw him across the room. There he was: talking to a leggy blonde in a long black dress who was hanging on to his every word with an expression of rapture on her face.

Just the sort of reaction he would expect as his due from a woman, Lizzy thought acidly, stabbing a prawn with her fork. And she had very nearly conformed to the role of bowled-over female, falling into his kiss like a sex-starved teenager!

Across the room, his eyes met hers and took in the cosy huddle. Lizzy met his narrowed stare defiantly. In fact, she found herself inching a little towards Freddy, the very picture of rapt interest in what was being said to her. Which, when she tuned in, was the tail end of something to do with the girl he had broken off with three weeks before.

Louis continued to stare at them over the rim of his glass as he sipped his wine, and with a toss of her head Lizzy looked away. But her nerves once again were all over the place and her mind had taken a crazy detour.

Was he going to sleep with the blonde tonight? They certainly looked good together: both tall, both striking, both with that invisible aura of self-confidence that always seemed to come naturally to those born with looks, grace and money.

A well-matched pair, in other words.

She was barely aware of Freddy, who had moved on from talking about his last girlfriend to a speculative conversation about Leigh—who had returned to the drawing room with an even more impressive entourage in tow. She appeared to be regaling them with tales of university life.

Lizzy suddenly felt exhausted. She wanted to go home and then she wanted to return to London. She wanted to feel the familiarity of her friends around her. Louis had challenged every inch of her comfort zone and she needed to return to a place where everything made sense.

Abruptly, she stood up and carefully placed her empty glass on the table, along with her plate. She vaguely noticed that Freddy seemed not in the least disconcerted by the fact that she had cut him off in mid-sentence and was preparing to go. His bright-blue eyes were focused elsewhere.

She left the room quickly, sidestepping her sisters, because Maisie had now joined Leigh and was triumphantly waving a bottle of champagne in the air to great cheers and laughter.

She didn't know where Louis had gone; he was no longer in the room. She wondered whether he was in another part of the house, getting close to the blonde—and thanking his lucky stars that he hadn't been foolish enough to lower himself into sleeping with a member of the grasping Sharp family, for whom he had nothing but disdain.

Hot, bothered and wrapped up in a hornet's nest of unpleasant, uninvited thoughts, she didn't see Louis. She should have because this time he hadn't stolen up on her from behind; he was right there in front of her. But her head was down and she was hurrying, and she crashed into him with such vigour that he had to reach out and steady her. His hands stayed in a vice-like grip on her arms until she was staring up at him, incapable of going anywhere.

CHAPTER SIX

HARD on the heels of Louis, appearing like a rabbit from a magician's hat, her mother materialised next to him. Lizzy hadn't spotted her mother all evening. From the looks of it, she had been having a grand time. Someone had stuck a hat on her head, which she was now sporting in a jaunty fashion, and she was beaming like a Cheshire cat—although the smile fell away when she spotted her daughter.

Lizzy firmly pushed Louis away and steadied herself.

'Where's Dad?' she asked in an accusing voice.

'He's helping himself to seconds. Fantastic food!' She turned her smile to Louis, who smiled back in polite acknowledgment of the compliment. 'Have you been drinking, Lizzy? You look a little green round the gills.'

Which provided her with the perfect excuse. 'I *do* feel a little under par, Mum…' She threw her mother a wan smile and ignored Louis who was standing on the sidelines, his arms folded, his eyebrows raised. 'And I don't want to drag anyone away from a good time, so I thought I might just take the car and head home. I'm sure you'll be able to cadge a lift back with the Robinsons, and Maisie and Leigh can fend for themselves; there are a hundred boys here who look like they would jump at the chance.'

'You're not leaving *already*, are you?' Her mother sounded as horrified as if she had just jumped on a table and begun a striptease. 'It's not even *midnight* yet!'

'There's no need for you to worry, Mrs Sharp.' Louis inserted himself smoothly into the conversation. 'If Lizzy isn't feeling well, then of course she must go home.'

Lizzy looked at him narrowly, torn between healthy suspicion and gratitude for getting her off the hook.

'And I would be delighted to deliver her back to your house in one piece. Or, of course,' he mused thoughtfully, turning to her, 'you *could* always stay here overnight. You're familiar with the layout of the house and I can make sure that you have the same room as you had last time. Naturally, it won't be quite as peaceful. There are a considerable number of people staying over.'

'I'm fine driving back.'

'Are you? You've been drinking.'

'So have you.'

'I've spent a lot of time nursing two drinks, interspersed with gallons of water.' He turned to Grace. 'I'm more than capable of driving your daughter home, leaving you all here to enjoy yourselves.'

Lizzy plastered a stiff smile on her face while she made her excuses to Rose and Nicholas. She was the first guest to leave; she could feel Jessica's eyes stonily watching her as she and Louis disappeared from the party.

'There was no need.' She turned to him as soon as they were outside. Even with her cape wrapped cosily around her, she could still feel the bitter, crisp cold.

She wasn't telling him anything he didn't already know. Louis knew that he was acting wildly out of character, but for the first time in living memory something other than pure, cold reason had motivated his behaviour.

Lizzy Sharp made no sense on every count. He had descended on Crossfeld with the aim of firstly checking out his investment—even though the detailed reports sent to him already guaranteed a successful venture, even with the money that needed to be poured into it. Secondly, and more importantly, on checking out Rose Sharp.

He had checked out Rose Sharp. He had checked out her family background and their financial situation. He had watched, and his conclusions were right. Rose Sharp, as per the entire family, was primarily motivated by the considerable advancement to her status that marriage to Nicholas would entail. Even if there was something about the girl that was so genuine that it beggared belief.

Why would Lizzy Sharp be anything else? She was stubborn and mouthy—which he normally wouldn't have associated with someone who wanted to worm her way towards anyone's bank balance—but the fact remained that she was part of the Sharp family. He should have cornered her with his suspicions and then left it alone. But he hadn't been able to. For reasons he couldn't begin to deduce, she had got under his skin, even though it was a distraction he really didn't need.

Lord, it wasn't as though there weren't enough women who would have been more than happy to fill his bed if he wanted.

But his mind, for once, was at odds with his body. He had done very little but watch her during the course of the evening, and when he had found himself alone with her in the conservatory he had been unable to control the impulse to kiss her. The fact that she had responded had fired up something in him that had not seen the light of day for a long time.

'I really don't want you driving me home,' Lizzy persisted in the face of his silence.

'No, you would have happily taken to the unlit roads in the depths of winter whilst over the limit. It's the same reckless selfishness that made you take to the road in blizzard conditions on a motorbike.'

Lizzy's nerves at having to sit alongside him in the close confines of a car, disappeared at this blatant insult, although a little voice in her head was telling her that he was absolutely right: there was no defence against his argument. So she pressed her lips together and stared fixedly ahead in silence, her pulses thrumming with tension as his silent Range Rover ate up the miles between Crossfeld and her parents' house.

'I take it you have a key to get in?' Her moody silence had been a tonic for Louis. An expert at reading other people, he could only deduce that she was finding it difficult to deal with his presence. So difficult, in fact, that she had temporarily lost her will to argue with him. He liked the thought of that. He liked the fact that he was getting to her, because she was getting to him—big time.

'Key?'

'House key.'

'Damn it. No; doesn't matter. You can leave me here. I can still get in, because we always keep a key under a flower pot at the side of the house.'

Louis had no intention of doing any such thing. 'Leave you here? I was brought up to always see a woman to the door.'

'Fine. You can stay in the car and watch me walk to the door.'

'You can take this as a compliment when I tell you that your sense of humour is growing on me.' He followed her to the front door, waiting and watching with amusement as she fumbled under a flower pot and retrieved a little bag containing the house key.

'Thank you for the lift, Louis.' Lizzy forced herself to smile, although her mind was in slow rewind, remembering the feel of his mouth against hers and the way his hand had confidently found the soft swell of her breast. 'There's really no need to see me in.'

'But what if there's an intruder inside waiting for you?' He pushed the door and held it open with his hand, allowing her just enough room to slide past him, and then stepping into the blessedly warm hallway.

The house bore evidence of robust family life. Shoes

adorned the bottom of the wide staircase. The Oriental rug, like the solid wooden floor underneath it, was worn with use, but not unattractive for that. From where he was, he could glimpse the end of the long pine table in the kitchen and the old-fashioned tiles on the floor which were now back in fashion. This was the house that the family would find them-selves losing, thanks to Adrian Sharp's overspending and poor investments. Little wonder they were desperate to hang on to it by hook or by crook.

Lizzy left him standing in the hallway and headed towards the kitchen. More than anything else, she wanted a cup of coffee. She would have to offer him one. He didn't look as though he was in any hurry to leave and she couldn't see how she could push him out. He was bigger, taller and stronger than she was.

'I can see why your parents are so keen on a match with Nicholas and his bank balance,' Louis drawled, startling her, because she hadn't heard him follow her into the kitchen. 'I suspect the last thing they want is to lose the family home.'

'Would you like a cup of coffee? I'm making one for myself, so it's no bother.' There was no way that she was going to be drawn into this familiar argument, although when she looked at him he was smiling at her with no sign of that cold hostility in his eyes. It was disconcerting. Somewhere between hall and kitchen, he had shed his coat and he looked rakishly, sinfully sexy. What would he look like under those expensive, tailored clothes? Lizzy squashed the thought and looked away hurriedly but her hand was shaking a little as she handed him the mug of coffee: black, no sugar. She had seen him drink coffee once, and already her brain had stored the insignificant detail of how he took it.

'I saw you whispering with Freddy.' Louis sat on one of the kitchen chairs and sipped his coffee. He hadn't liked it. For the first time he admitted that he had been jealous, had had to restrain himself from marching over like a feudal master and breaking up the little confab.

'We were chatting, yes. I happen to like him.'

'Chatting about what?'

'None of your business.'

'If you're thinking about getting involved with him, then I'm warning you not to bother. Freddy is only interested in women who have sufficient money to keep him in the style to which he thinks he's entitled.'

'How did I know you'd say that? You always see the worst in everyone!'

'And, if he's interested in one of your sisters, then I would pass the warning on if I were you. He might have fun with them for a while, but he'll walk away without a backward glance the minute it suits him.'

'Because they're broke students without a family pile and an inheritance?'

Louis shrugged. Her cheeks were pink and she was leaning forward, glaring at him. His eyes drifted to her full mouth, currently compressed with anger.

'He likes women with money and plenty of it.'

'Isn't that the pot calling the kettle black?' Lizzy snapped and was gratified when his face darkened.

'Where are you going with that?'

'Where do you think?' Lizzy muttered under her breath. She was aware that she might have pushed the boundaries a little too far this time but she wasn't going to back down. Quite.

'To use an old-fashioned term, Freddy is a cad.'

'Funny, but that's exactly what he said about you.' She gave a little squeak of dismay as the words shot out of her mouth and hung tensely between them.

'So that's what your cosy *tête à tête* was all about,' Louis murmured. 'You were in a huddle talking about me. I didn't think I was that fascinating a topic of conversation.'

'You're not.'

'What did he have to say about me? I expect he spun you the story of the money he was due that never came his way because I'm the big, bad, greedy wolf?'

Lizzy had never been a gossip, yet here she was—mortified—because, not only had she gossiped madly about Louis, she had enjoyed it. What would he think of her? she wondered. Of course, it didn't matter *what* he thought of her, but still…

'I don't normally talk about people behind their back,' she said by way of grudging apology, and was surprised when his eyes lingered on her flushed face thoughtfully.

'No, I don't suppose you do.'

'I… I was annoyed with you and Freddy was there.'

The jealousy that had gripped Louis was fading fast; *this* he could deal with.

'And, yes, he did say something about being done out of money that was due to him.'

'Interested in hearing the other side of the story? Or would that risk you having to see my point of view for a change?' He caught her eye, held it and then watched in some fascination as she pensively chewed her lower lip.

'I'll interpret that silence as a yes,' Louis said drily, draining the last of his coffee and standing up. 'Freddy's father was a very good, very loyal and very faithful family retainer.' He held up one hand, as though she had said something. 'And let's not get sidetracked by the rights and wrongs of families who have retainers. I agree that it's an outdated custom, but spare a thought for the fact that it also provides an extremely comfortable job for life. The families of retainers being looked after is also a handy perk for them.

'Samuel always worried about his son. The older Freddy got, the wilder he became, and my father promised that whatever happened he would be financially looked after. I think he hoped that somewhere along the line between puberty and manhood Freddy would straighten himself out, but he never did. When my father died, he left a codicil in his will that Freddy be taken care of financially at such time that it became necessary, and that any money handed over would be at my discretion. When Samuel died three years later, it was my duty to decide what to do.'

Louis raked restless fingers through his hair and shot her a dark, brooding look from under his lashes.

He had been prowling around the kitchen, absentmindedly taking in the bottle-green double-fronted aga and all the paraphernalia of a well-used kitchen. Now he paused to stand in front of her and Lizzy looked up at him, guiltily aware that she had been eager to hear one side of a story, and would have left it there because it suited her ends to clutch on to something that placed Louis squarely in a poor light. He was so tall that she had to lean back into her chair to look at him. His hands were in his pockets and he looked absolutely and completely at ease, although she could *sense* the angry tension radiating out of him in silent, invisible waves.

'Freddy was right—there was no way I could give him a wad of money and then let him loose to get on with it. He was dabbling in recreational drugs at the time. I took the view that handing him over any money at all might encourage a habit. Instead, I stuck him in rehab and then offered him a job at one of my companies. Needless to say, he was never that thankful for the opportunity to earn an honest crust. Not when he had always expected to be given a lump sum to squander.'

Lizzy flushed and lowered her eyes. Now, instead of looking at the beautiful, hard angles of his face, she was confronted by his black, polished shoes and his trouser legs. The tailored cloth outlined his muscular thighs to perfection and was almost as disconcerting.

'He goes to the office on an occasional basis,' Louis continued. Lizzy thought that he was remarkably phlegmatic about the situation, all things considered. 'I keep a check on him through my people there. I wasn't surprised when he showed up at the restaurant in search of a handout.'

'You weren't?'

'I knew he'd been spending way over his limit. I also knew where the money had gone.'

'And you don't mind?'

'Of course I mind. But I have a duty of honour. Freddy's expenditures are a necessary write-off as far as I'm concerned—within reason, naturally. And just so long as no money gets spent on drugs.' He leaned over her, supporting himself on the arms of the wooden carver-chair. 'But this all brings me back to Freddy and what he looks for in women. I don't target women because they have money—Freddy does. Let him in, and he'll break your heart.'

'Break *my* heart?' Lizzy laughed for the first time, a rich, full sound that went straight to Louis's head like a goblet of the finest red wine drunk on an empty stomach. 'No chance.'

'Really? He has a high strike-rate with the opposite sex. That little-boy-in-need-of-care-and-attention look works wonders, I gather.'

'Not with me,' she said scornfully. When she glanced down, she could see his fine, dark hair curling over the dull silver of his watch strap where the sleeves of his shirt had ridden up.

'No. You like them thoughtful and caring.'

'That's right.' But her voice faltered, and with the instincts of a born predator Louis picked up on that infinitesimal hesitation with something that tasted of victory.

'You don't sound convinced,' he offered, and Lizzy looked at him helplessly. 'I agree,' he murmured, pinning her with his amazing eyes and hypnotising her with the soft, velvety drawl of his voice. 'Thoughtful and caring are traits that sound great on paper, but in practice? Well, not exactly scintillating, are they? Thoughtful, caring guys might cook a great meal and offer to do the vacuuming, but do they really set the bed ablaze?'

'They, er, I don't know where you're going with this.'

'Where would you like me to go with it?'

A steady drum beat began in her head. She was straining up to him with every fibre of her being. Her body was obeying its own rules now, so that when she found herself reaching up and stroking the side of his face with her fingers it felt like a disembodied gesture. Someone else was doing that, just as it was someone else's hand that was being caught by his and turned over so that he could press his mouth against the soft palm.

'Like that?' Louis kept his mouth against her hand so that she felt the warmth of his breath when he spoke, but he was looking at her with a crooked smile that made her shiver.

'You should go…'

'Where would you like me to go?'

The tantalising, wicked suggestion hung in the air between them and suddenly Lizzy felt reckless. While Rose had been busy being traditional and looking pretty, Vivian had been busy saving the world, and Maisie and Leigh had been busy just being Maisie and Leigh, she had been busy pretending that she was the free thinker in the family—the unique one who didn't give a damn about looks or about what other people thought of her. She could ride her motorbike, work in an inner-city school in London, wear whatever she wanted to wear and she certainly would never waste her time trying to be sexy for the sake of a guy. Especially not for the sake of a guy who was as far out of reach for someone like her as the man on the moon.

But there was no denying Louis did something to her. He made her keenly, stupidly aware of herself as a woman, and when he had kissed her he had left her wanting much more. And more than that; he was no cardboard cut-out she could write off with a toss of her head. He was clever, sharp and witty and, judging from what he had said about Freddy, scrupulously fair. She wasn't attracted to him because of the way he looked. She was attracted to the whole package—and it scared the life out of her.

So, in answer to his question, the appropriate words—*out of the house, of course, and as far away from me as you can possibly get*—were not the ones that sprang to mind.

'You're going to have to tell me, you know, Lizzy,' Louis said conversationally. 'Because I don't make it a habit to force myself on anyone.'

'You shouldn't have kissed me.'

'Maybe you shouldn't have enjoyed it so much.'

Lizzy stood up on wobbly legs and walked towards the kitchen door, then she threw him a look over her shoulder. Louis had never in his entire life seen anything so sexy. Her long, dark hair tumbled in vibrant disarray over one shoulder. She had kicked off her shoes in the hallway, and there was something mind-blowingly erotic and yet weirdly innocent about the suggestive dress twinned with her bare, stockinged feet.

Her bedroom was upstairs at the far end of the house. As with what he had seen downstairs, up here bore evidence of young women: an odd, high-heeled shoe lying in the corridor, and through the open doors he passed he could see two dressing-tables that could barely be seen underneath the riot of make-up.

But Lizzy's room, when they got there and she switched on the little lamp on the chest of drawers, was surprisingly tidy. He felt himself smile at the motorcycle helmet on the chair by the window.

Lizzy, looking at him as he cast his eyes over her room, felt exposed and vulnerable, and for one frantic moment she wondered what on earth she was doing here, with him, in her bedroom. At least, she *knew* what she was doing; she just briefly wondered *why*.

With a sigh of desperate longing, she reached behind her to unzip her dress, but she didn't get as far as pulling the zipper halfway down before he was standing in front of her, making her tremble with the intensity of his gaze.

'No way.'

'But I thought…' Lizzy began.

'I mean, no way are *you* going to undress yourself. That's a pleasure that's reserved for *me*.' He liked the way she quivered as he very slowly unzipped the dress; there was no coy giggling or attempt to smoulder as he pulled it down. She just stepped out of it and stood there in a simple cotton bra, some matching pants and her sensible tights. He had told her that he was going to undress her and she was taking him at his word, her stillness a turn-on beyond belief.

Louis wondered how long he had been thinking of doing this. Certainly the second he had kissed her in that conservatory, he had known that he had started something that would have to be finished. But playing on the edges of his mind was the suspicion that he had been thinking of her for a while before that.

He unclasped her bra, and this time she gave a soft gasp as her breasts were exposed to his admiring eyes. It was an effort to control himself as he looked at the full swell and the rosy, pouting nipples.

'Now you're not to move a muscle,' he whispered to her. 'I want you to just stand and enjoy…'

Lizzy nodded, because actually she didn't think that she could articulate anything coherent. Her tongue seemed to be stuck to the roof of her mouth and, Lord, it felt downright decadent to be standing like a statue with her bra off and her breasts aching to be touched. She knew that he was going to get to that, and the anticipation coursed through her bloodstream like a powerful drug.

She looked down as he knelt like a supplicant in front of her and slowly eased off the tights, which she stepped out of. Then, when her underwear followed suit, she had to fight to control her breathing. She squeezed her eyes tightly shut and gasped out loud when she felt his tongue slip into her moistness, gently and slickly darting against the throbbing bud of her femininity; teasing her until she could no longer maintain her statue pose, but instead had to clasp her hands into his dark hair and open her legs to accommodate his questing mouth.

It felt so good that she wanted to splinter into a thousand pieces. It should have been an invasion of her body. This was a private part of her that no one had ever touched before—certainly not in the way he was now touching her—but it didn't feel like an invasion, it felt shockingly right, and she caved in to the pleasure of having him taste her.

When she felt as though she could no longer resist being tipped over the edge, Louis stood up. His body was so close to hers that she could feel the hardness of his erection pressing against her through his trousers.

While he ravaged her mouth with his, she fumbled and finally succeeded in undoing the zip of his trousers. Then it was her turn to take control as she took his erection in her hand, and started doing things to him that made his big body shudder and drove him to plunder her mouth with even more hunger.

With a groan, Louis swept her off her feet and carried her to the bed, depositing her there, and then getting out of his clothes while she watched in frank and open appreciation.

He had the muscular, well-toned body of an athlete. She said, impulsively, 'I bet you work out all the time. Do you?'

'When I get the chance.' Louis grinned down at her up-turned face which, in the mellow light cast by the lamp on the chest of drawers, was like that of a kid in a toyshop. 'There's a gym in the building; I use it whenever I can. Is that your way of telling me that you like what you see?'

'It's passable.'

'That's not much of a compliment. Now I'm going to have to try and persuade you that it's a lot more than that by showing you what I can do with it.'

He hadn't dared risk looking at her nakedness as she lay on the bed in front of him, one arm flung over her head with abandon. Now he did. Her body was as smooth as satin and boyish in build: slim hips, a flat stomach and rounded breasts that tempted him with their large, pink nipples, that begged to be taken into his mouth and suckled until she was driven mad with pleasure.

All in good time. Right now, he wanted to fill his eyes with the beauty of her. He reached out and gently pushed her legs apart and he had to hold down his painful erection with his hand as they obligingly fell open, leaving his imagination free to run wild.

Her hand fluttered over one breast and that marked the time for his inspection to be over. Looking at her was more than his body could stand, and he joined her on the bed and pulled her roughly to him so that he could kiss her—a demanding, hungry kiss that had her writhing against him and curving her leg over his thigh where she moved her body against his pulsing erection.

'Ever had a man talk dirty to you?' Louis asked huskily and she giggled with a mixture of pleasure and genuine shock.

'Of course not!'

'Then let me educate on what I'd like to do with your body...'

Which he proceeded to do, in between the glorious business of attending to her breasts, sucking on her nipples until they were wet and throbbing, and attending to all those other parts of her body, from her stomach to her belly button, and finally to that place that was still aching for him.

Through lowered lashes Lizzy feverishly watched his dark head between her legs, tasting her and licking her, bringing her up to his mouth by the very expedient method of placing his big hands firmly under her buttocks.

He was buried between her thighs. The only sounds were those of their love-making. Her legs were crossed over his broad back and she surrendered to the insistent pressure of his tongue as it explored every inch of her, circling and tickling the sensitised nub before moving downwards, only to return to torment her.

When she began to buck, he finally surfaced and said, 'No way...'

But before he actually came into her, there was one more question: 'I haven't got any contraception with me. Are you safe?'

Lizzy nodded, and it was no lie; she had been on the pill for the past six months. Not because of a raunchy sex life— or *any* sex life, for that matter—but to reduce the stomach cramps that attacked her monthly. In between her urgency for him slipped a disquieting thought: *what if she hadn't been? Would he have stopped? Because an unwanted pregnancy would have been his nightmare.* But the thought had no time to take root because he was entering her, and the second she felt the weight of him easing inside her there was no room left in her head for any thoughts at all.

She had been brought so close to the edge that it took only a couple of thrusts. The same must have been true for him, she dimly thought with satisfaction, for they both came with a wrenching intensity that left them spent.

'I can normally hold out for longer.' Louis turned on his side and propped himself on his elbow to look down at her. Her face was flushed and damp with perspiration and her bare breast, resting like ripened fruit against his hand, was already beginning to stir his senses. With a grunt of surprise—because his body had never responded with such immediate ease after he had made love—he shifted a little and stroked some hair away from her face.

'Show off,' Lizzy teased. 'Maybe it's because you find me so irresistible.'

'There's a thought.'

But although he was smiling he didn't expand on that, which was a little disappointing.

'You're going to have to go,' she told him, wishing with all her heart that she was anywhere but under the roof of her parents' house, because she didn't want him to leave. Not when they were like this, wrapped around each other without sufficient space between their bodies to wedge a credit card. 'I don't know what time it is, but my family are all going to be back soon.'

'Shame.' Louis guided her hand to where he was already hardening for her.

'Not fair,' Lizzy whispered. *Are you going to see me again or am I your wrong-side-of-the-tracks one-night stand?*

'True. But you're right; I'm going to have to go before they send out a search party.' He reluctantly eased himself off the bed and without bothering to get dressed grabbed her towel from where it was hanging over the back of a chair and disappeared, in search of a shower.

It should have given her vital time to get her thoughts in order. She knew she had to. But instead she just lay there, still breathing in the scent of him lingering on the sheets, and waited for him to come back, which he did after only a few minutes.

There was no pride left as she watched him put on his clothes, then he came to sit on the side of the bed, his weight causing the mattress to dip.

'I'm going to be heading back to London first thing in the morning.'

'Right.'

Louis waited for her to ask him if he would be in touch, but she didn't, which made him smile; if there was one woman on the face of the earth who seemed to have the power to make him jump through hoops, then it surely must be this one. 'I don't have your mobile number.' He flipped out his phone to put her in his address book and frowned when his request was met was silence.

Should she pretend that this was anything but a romp in the sack? Lizzy wondered. So she gave him her mobile number; then what? Try as she might to jettison her natural prejudice, she still couldn't help but think that he was a one-way ticket to heartbreak. But surely, she thought, chewing her lips and staring off into the distance, her heart wasn't his to break? And why should she let a sense of caution hold her back from an amazing sexual adventure—something she had never done in her entire life? What was so wrong about behaving out of character just this once? They connected on an instinctive level that blew away all her defences, and she liked that.

'I suppose I *could* give it to you…' She dragged out the sentence, thinking all the while and not noticing his deepening frown.

Poised to type it in, Louis was staggered that he was actually waiting for the number of a woman who might possibly not want to follow up on what they had just enjoyed. Worse, a woman with whom he should have so little in common as to be laughable. But, when she finally rattled it off, he typed it in and clicked shut his phone with something like relief.

'When are you back in London?' He traced the outline of her nipple with his finger, and she moaned softly and tapped away his hand. 'I'll call you.'

'Okay. If you like.' Lizzy sat up and pulled the quilt right up to cover her body. It was crazy, but she wanted to hang on to him like a limpet and never let him go. 'I'll be back at the beginning of next week.'

'I can't wait.' His dark eyes held hers until she felt like she was drowning. Then he was on his feet, walking towards the bedroom door, leaving with just one backward glance and a satisfied nod of his head.

CHAPTER SEVEN

Louis found the school easily and was there now, sitting in his car with the engine off, trying to get his bearings. The place had the look of a miniature prison, especially at five-thirty in mid-winter with the few trees bare of leaves and groups of straggling pupils lurking in small groups outside. He was beginning to understand why she had roared with laughter when he had suggested visiting the school, should he decide to make a donation to its coffers. Regrets were surfacing over his decision to come in his Maserati.

He mentally shrugged to himself because there was no point getting stressed out over what couldn't be changed and he certainly wasn't about to drive back to his office without seeing her.

He had spent his entire time abroad in restless anticipation of when they would next meet. When he was away on business, women never crossed his mind, even when he had one waiting back in London for him. He never called because, quite literally, he never thought about them. For Lizzie, he had found himself making the exception, on several occasions and with increasing frustration when he couldn't get through. Her mobile either rang and rang until he was obliged to give up or else he was immediately connected to voicemail.

Unbelievably, he had set a ferociously gruelling pace on his meetings and arrived back in the UK two days ahead of schedule. At some point, he had come to the conclusion that she was avoiding him. It was almost unthinkable but, once it surfaced, the thought took root and refused to go away.

He told himself that if she was playing a game then she would be the inevitable loser, because there was nothing he hated more than someone thinking that they could generate his interest by playing hard to get. He reminded himself that she was hardly long-term-relationship material; he was just too wary of anyone who could conceivably see him as a meal ticket and she certainly fitted that category whether she liked to admit it or not. He had concluded that his best course of action would be to walk away.

And then he had touched down at Heathrow, gone to his apartment, showered and promptly driven to her place of work. Pride seemed to have taken a back seat, and see her he would. He was in possession of his cheque book; she would have no choice *but* to see him. What school in need of funds could afford to turn away someone with a cheque book?

And the school, from everything he could see as he headed for the reception area, could do with a few charitable donations. Underneath the array of school posters and notices, the paint was peeling. The little collection of hand-made *papier mâché* sculptures cordoned off to the side was desperately trying to inject some cheer but seemed to be losing the battle against the dour surroundings.

It was a far cry from the top-notch boarding school he had attended, where everything had gleamed with the patina of loving care and attention thanks to a school fund bursting at the seams with money.

Already he was attracting interested looks, and by the time he made it to the staff room, after a couple of wrong turnings, he was alert to the fact that he was in unknown territory. A life of privilege had cushioned him against the grimmer realities of life.

To a man, the staff room fell quiet as he strolled in and stood by the door, his eyes flicking around the box room with its battered coffee-machine and tired arrangement of mismatched chairs interspersed amongst the desks, some of which sported computers but most of which did not.

'I'm looking for a teacher here. Lizzy Sharp.'

'She's outside on playground duty for the kids who aren't being collected until later.' The oldest of the women there stood up and approached him. She had a warm, friendly face and a cloud of reddish-brown hair that had obviously started life as a bun but in the space of a frazzled day had evolved to a messy arrangement of straggling strands hurriedly clipped back. 'And you are…? I don't recognise you as being a parent.'

'I'm…eh…a friend.' There was a round of giggles from the room and Louis flushed and shifted on his feet. 'We were discussing a possible donation to the school.' This had the effect of killing the titters and the level of interest tangibly altered. Suddenly and unexpectedly, he was bombarded with a series of enthusiastic suggestions as to where any possible money could be spent, and he had a fleeting notion of why Lizzy enjoyed her working life so much. She was as passionate as this lot. She wasn't into playing games; why had he ever thought that? Which meant that she was avoiding him, actively avoiding him, and it occurred to him that she was avoiding him because he really just wasn't the kind of guy she either wanted or needed in her life.

He glanced around the room for any men who might be candidates for her affection but the three men were all in their mid-forties; there was no one. The irony of her prejudices struck him like a blow to the stomach. On and on she went about *his* outdated snobbishness while she was willing to jettison *him* because of *her* outdated stereotyping!

'If you point me in the right direction…' He held his hand up to signify silence. 'I want to chat to her before I commit to anything.'

'I'll take you to the playground. I'm Mrs Evans, by the

way…' The woman who had first approached him held out her hand by way of introduction and gave him a surprisingly firm handshake. 'I'm the deputy head. And this rabble here…' she grinned at all the other teachers '…are my mostly hard-working team.' Which was met with cries of laughter and protest. 'They're a wonderful crew,' she confided as she led him away. 'And Lizzy is really a wonderfully talented teacher. The kids adore her and as you can see from the surroundings…' she gestured to encompass the school '…many of them come from disadvantaged backgrounds, so a firm bond with their teacher is really important.'

Louis had a vivid image of these corridors crowded with stampeding kids. The conditions were far from inspiring, although every class he passed showed the valiant efforts of all the teachers to make up for the crumbling building. No wall was left unadorned.

They reached the playground and he turned to the deputy head with a smile. 'If you don't mind, I'll just wait here a while before I go out—think about, eh, any possible donation and how the…discussion should proceed. Naturally, nothing will be decided without first consulting you and the principal.'

Which left him standing in the shadow of the doorway out to the playground, an unobserved spectator watching with keen interest the slight figure with the woollen hat firmly pulled down who was laughing and chivvying fifteen or so kids into some kind of game—which was clearly hilarious from the looks of it. He looked on as two of the smaller children ran towards her and she stooped down so that she was on their level and pulled one of the kids towards her for a hug.

He had no idea how long he remained standing there, watching her, but eventually he pushed himself away from the wall and headed in her direction. She didn't notice him coming, and even when he was standing right in front of her it took her a few seconds to register that he wasn't a parent.

Even in the barely-there lighting he saw the muscles in her face tighten as she stood up and brushed herself down.

'What are you doing here?'

'I've been trying to get through to you. Why haven't been taking my calls?'

'Why do you think?'

'If I knew, I wouldn't be standing here asking you the question.'

'You have to go. I'm busy, and anyway we have nothing to talk about.'

'I don't think your charming Mrs Evans would be too impressed if you sent me away. Not when I've already told her that I'm thinking of making a donation to the school. A very generous donation.'

'If you've come to talk about a donation, then you should be talking to her or to the principal. You can make an appointment.'

'God, Lizzy.' Louis raked his fingers impatiently through his hair. 'What the hell is going on with you? The last time I left you we'd just made love and were planning to see each other again. What happened in the meantime?'

Lizzy looked at him mutinously, her mouth downturned. 'I don't want to talk about this—and I can't here, anyway. As you can see, I'm busy. I can't afford to take my eyes off this lot for a second.'

'In that case I'll wait here with you.'

'Okay. In *that* case, you can help.' She didn't give him time to consider that option. She clapped her hands and before he could object, she had managed to rope him into a schoolyard game that involved him having to run, having to hop, having to shout and having to look absolutely ridiculous in his expensive black cashmere coat and patent-leather shoes.

Except that he managed to pull it off—and take it one step further. He was giving orders, arranging them into neat little groups and making up a game of his own that had them entranced. What, she thought sourly, were the chances of *that*?

'So…' Louis walked over to her after the last small child had been collected and she was busily getting the playground back into order. 'Are you going to tell me what's going on or are you going to put me to another test? Enrol me to teach your most disruptive class tomorrow?' She turned around to go and he caught her by her arm and pulled her towards him. 'You *are* going to talk to me, you know.'

'Or else what? The school misses out on your "maybe, maybe not" donation?'

'I'm not that infantile. Is there somewhere close by we could go for something to drink?'

Lizzy looked at him, knowing that he wouldn't go away. Had she expected him to turn up when she had ignored all his calls? No. But, now that he was here, she couldn't suppress that familiar excitement that undermined all her good intentions.

'There's a pub at the corner.' She turned away, desperate to create space between them, and conscious of him right behind her as she returned to the staff room. She tried to pin a smile on her face as he chatted to Laura Evans about the donation and made an appointment to return the following week.

Half an hour later, with a glass of white wine in front of her, she was still as jittery as when she had first looked up and seen him staring down at her as though he had stepped straight out of her imagination and materialised in front of her by force of magic.

'How was your trip?' she asked thinly, every muscle in her body rigid with tension.

'You might have known had you picked your phone up.' Louis sipped his beer and watched her carefully. She was dressed for school: trousers, flat shoes, a baggy jumper and hair tied back in braids that made her look like a teenager. As far away from the glamorous woman at the party at Crossfeld as it was possible to be and yet just as alluring.

'Well, you succeeded. You must be pleased.' She drank half of the contents of her glass in one gulp and her stomach burned in immediate response.

'What are you talking about?' Caught on the back foot by the same sort of direct approach he himself was accustomed to taking, Louis could only look at her in bewilderment, which had the effect of making her give a short, dry bark of laughter.

'Take a guess.'

'I don't do guessing games.'

'Have you spoken to Nicholas since you got back?'

'Get to the point.'

'Don't give me orders!'

'You are the most challenging bloody woman I have *ever* met in my *entire* life!'

'I'll take that as a compliment if it means that you don't walk all over me like you do everyone else.'

'You've lost me.'

'You went to Crossfeld with a mission to break up my sister and Nicholas because you thought that he was too good for her. Well, congratulations—you've succeeded.' She polished off the rest of the wine and glared at him with angry resentment.

'Explain.' There was nothing to explain; that was exactly why he had made that arduous trip when he had. But, still, knowing that he had managed to succeed tasted like a hollow victory.

Rose hadn't been the disagreeable, conniving gold-digger he had expected to find. Try as he had—and he *had* tried very hard—he had found himself warming to her even when his head told him that he was being a fool. He was a man of facts and figures, and the facts and figures had added up to a woman on the lookout for a man with a healthy bank

balance. Hell, she hadn't even seemed all that much in love
with Nicholas at the beginning. But he had seen those looks
she had shared with Nicholas and there had been no pretence
there. Even when he had been declaring his scepticism to
Lizzy, he had already been walking away from a task in which
he had less and less conviction.

'Does it matter?' She was finding him unnerving. It was
also unnerving the way her body was reacting to him as a lover
instead of as an antagonist, which she had spent the past few
days telling herself that she was. Eventually she shrugged. 'A
couple of days after you left, Rose came home in floods of
tears. She had gone to Crossfeld House to find your wonderful
girlfriend there with her sister, about to pack and leave.'

'Jessica?'

'Who else?'

'I won't waste my breath telling you what you must already
know. She was never my girlfriend and she isn't my girlfriend
now. She's the sister of a close friend, and frankly a woman
I could never envisage having in my life in anything like
an intimate relationship. Although, please do feel free to be
consumed with jealousy.'

Sensing the direction of the conversation, Louis's voice was
laced with biting sarcasm, although when he thought about her
being jealous about him he felt a curious kick. Her jealousy
was something he really would have enjoyed, although it was
a trait he had always abhorred in other women.

'I'm not jealous. I'm…I'm… No; I'm not disgusted. It was
probably what I should have expected from you all along.
You never gave Rose a chance, but I'm really disappointed
that Nicholas couldn't see for himself how much she was in
love with him. I'm really disappointed that when it came to
the crunch he decided that you were right. What does it feel
like to have that much influence over someone else? Does it
make you feel powerful? How does it feel to know that you've
ruined my sister's life?'

'You're blowing this out of all proportion.'

'Don't you dare say that!'

'What did Jessica say to your sister? No—hold that thought. I'm going to get you another drink.'

Lizzy opened her mouth to protest because she was anything but a drinker, but the thought of that pleasantly numbing effect caused by the wine was enticing. She watched, her nerves all over the place as he stood by the bar commanding attention in that way he had—the same way he had managed to command attention from a bunch of random seven- and eight-year-old kids he had never met in his life before who were, generally speaking, distrustful of any adult figure of authority they didn't know. It was just the way he was.

'Now. Talk to me.' He sat back and looked at her while Lizzy cradled the wine glass in her hands and stared down at the gently swirling liquid.

'I honestly don't see the point of going into all of this.'

'Humour me.'

'Jessica told her that Nicholas had decided to leave Crossfeld. He had finished everything he had set out to do and there was no need for him to remain any longer. He hadn't said a word to Rose about leaving. She just showed up in the morning to find that he had disappeared.'

Louis's mouth tightened. It didn't take much imagination to figure out what Jessica's take on that would have been. Far more than Eloise, she had disapproved of her brother going out with 'a nobody', as she had described Rose.

'It's not like Nicholas to behave like that.'

'It might be, considering you and his entire family had been working on him for the entire time you were at Crossfeld!'

'We've been through this.'

'So are you saying that you met Rose, saw for yourself what kind of person she was and so decided to take back everything you had said to Nicholas about not throwing his hat in the ring with a gold-digger?'

Louis looked at her with some discomfort. It was an emotion he was not accustomed to feeling but neither could he lie about the situation.

'Didn't think so,' Lizzy said bitterly. At the back of her mind there played even more miserable and humiliating thoughts of what else Jessica had said to Rose.

'Has your sister been able to get through to Nicholas or has she just spoken to Jessica?'

'What's the point of her calling Nicholas? Anyway, she's not much up to doing anything at the moment. She's gone back to her job, and it's best for her to put the whole thing behind her and get on with her life. There's nothing to be gained from pining for a guy who was never really interested in a serious relationship.'

'So speaks the voice of wisdom. In case you're interested, I might have spoken to Nicholas when I first arrived at Crossfeld, but after that I left it to him to make his mind up about what choices he wanted. I might look out for his welfare, but I'm not into running other people's lives.'

'Are you telling me that *I* am?' Lizzy shot him a fulminating look from under her lashes and scowled.

The woolly hat was off and her hair was all over the place from where she had yanked it. Her huge brown eyes were narrowed on him with antipathy and her full lips were thinned into a line of disapproval. Still Louis was fascinated by her face, by the angle of her slender body as she leaned towards him, by the way she managed to spit self-righteous fury yet look sexy at the same time. Was that why he was finding it hard to obey his natural instincts and walk away from this scene? He hated scenes; he loathed histrionics of any kind.

'Jessica said that Nicholas is destined to marry your sister. Apparently it's been an understanding for years.'

'Nicholas? Marry Giselle?' Louis was momentarily distracted from the temptation to smooth that unruly hair away from her face, even if he risked getting his hand slapped away for doing it.

'She also knows…knows that you and I… About us.'

Louis stilled and his fabulous eyes narrowed onto her unsmiling, flushed face. 'She told you this, did she?'

'She told Rose. Poor Rose didn't have a clue what to say. She was really thrown into the thick of it. Did you tell Jessica about us?' That had been playing on her mind for days. Had he and Jessica shared a confidential little chat about her behind her back? The look of stunned incredulity on his face killed any such notion and she felt slightly ashamed for having thought of it in the first place.

'I'm insulted that that should ever have even crossed your mind.'

Lizzy blushed and shot him a defiant look which he met head-on until she muttered a reluctant apology.

'What's that? I can't hear you.'

'I suppose I might have mistakenly suspected the worst of you,' she admitted grudgingly, playing with the end of her braid, twirling it round nervous fingers. 'But you can't blame me.'

'And that would be because…?' Louis sighed impatiently. 'Freddy Dale spins you a woeful yarn about an inheritance I've supposedly contrived to steal from him, and you believe him. Jessica sees fit to inform your sister that Nicholas has scarpered because he was just out to use her, and you blame me. Then she informs Rose that she knows about us, and you immediately think that I've told her.'

'Yes, well…' An unsettling realisation washed through her like a stirring tsunami. She felt safer blaming him, safer thinking the worst of him, because if she didn't then she would open a door to emotions she wouldn't know how to control. She had slept with him and she wasn't a girl who was into one-night stands. She had slept with him and it had felt right, because underneath all the bravado she was drawn to him in ways that terrified her. He made her feel alive. The second she had ground to a gravelly stop on that bleak, deserted road and interacted with him, she hadn't been able to get him out of her head. He had taken up residence there; it didn't make sense, but she couldn't fight it.

So what did that mean? Lizzy felt suddenly faint. She wouldn't contemplate having feelings for him. At least not *those* kind of feelings—the kind that grabbed you from behind and made you smile because the world was suddenly a bright place and anything was possible.

Those were the kind of feelings that were reserved for the guy she would eventually fall in love with.

'I should go,' she muttered with a sick sensation in the pit of her stomach.

'No way.'

'You can't tell me what to do!' But her voice lacked conviction.

'I seem to remember you enjoying it the last time I told you what to do.'

In bed. Lizzy went bright red. 'And that won't be happening again.'

'What won't?'

'Me. You. Us. In bed. That.'

'Because I've reverted to being the bad guy?'

'You were always the bad guy. Okay, maybe not as bad as I originally thought.' She was dismayed when he took her hand in his and began toying with her fingers. By the time she had got her wits about her sufficiently to snatch her hand away, she knew that it was just a token, transparent gesture, and he knew it, too, judging from the half-smile on his face.

'She told Rose that I was a complete idiot for getting involved with you,' Lizzy admitted in a rush. 'Not that I'm *involved* with you. But a fool for having slept with you. I had to drag that out of Rose, and she was as tactful as she could be with her replies, so I can't imagine how much more insulting

Jessica was face to face. She said that we might imagine ourselves to be something big in a tiny little, unimportant village in the middle of nowhere, but that there was no way that you would ever consider any kind of relationship with someone like me. Someone *like me*! She said that you and she had an understanding.'

Louis narrowed his eyes. Priority one as soon as he walked out of this place would be to sort Jessica out once and for all. He had been lenient with her, had tolerated her flirtatiousness, but her vendetta against the Sharp family had obviously mushroomed out of control.

'And even if you *don't* have an understanding,' Lizzy continued, gathering momentum now that she had started, 'I've decided that I don't want anything to do with you. Rose is out of Nicholas's life and I want you out of mine, which is why I didn't pick up any of your calls.'

She took a deep breath and willed herself to continue because now that she had started she would finish. 'I know that I'm attracted to you; I'm not going to deny that. But I've had time to sit and think and work out that I'm just not the sort who can throw herself into a passing fling just because the sex is good. And you're not the sort of guy who can throw himself into a full-fledged relationship, not with someone like me, even if the sex is good. You have that *perfect criteria* of yours and I'll never fit it. So we're at an impasse.'

Louis, only now surfacing from the task that lay ahead of dealing with Jessica, focused on the one word that really stuck in his throat and refused to budge: *impasse*. When it came to women, the thought of being rejected, as he had been at Lizzy's hands, was almost as unthinkable as the thought of her informing him that they had reached an impasse.

'Okay.'

'*Okay?*' Lizzy was utterly taken aback by the speed with which he had caved in to her long, heartfelt speech. He had been phoning and texting her every single day they had been apart. Good Lord, they had made love with tenderness and passion only about a week ago, and now here he was, acting as though it was no big deal that she was telling him that they couldn't go on. What did that mean?

'What else would you like me to say?' Louis asked smoothly. 'You've made your mind up and I respect that.'

'Good!'

He watched her bristle and knew that, whatever it was he wanted from this woman, his freedom wasn't one of those things—but he wasn't going to dwell on the why and where-fores of that conclusion. She still distrusted him and he could understand why. He would have to gain her trust; although he was adept at pretty much anything he cared to set his hand to, he suspected that his talents when it came to subtle and careful wooing might be a bit on the rusty side. They certainly hadn't been pulled out of the cupboard for as long as he could remember.

'Although I think you should know that I intend to phone Nicholas and find out what exactly is going on. I also intend to finally and conclusively set Jessica on the straight and narrow. Maybe,' he mused, 'I'll find her something to do in one of my companies. She's done nothing since she got her degree, and as we all know the devil makes work for idle hands.'

'You're going to have a word with *Nicholas*?'

'I'm not in the habit of accepting everything at face value. I intend to get to the bottom of his so-called desertion, if only for my own personal satisfaction.'

'You—you don't have to do that,' Lizzy stammered.

'Oh, but I do. And don't you think Rose would want to know? To hear the full story rather than the abbreviated Jessica version?'

'I...I think she's just focusing on getting on with her life now.'

'Because you told her that that would be the right thing to

do? Because you decided that pride was the most important thing at stake?'

'No!' Lizzy protested vehemently. She suddenly felt as though the solid ground beneath her feet had abruptly given way to quicksand. 'Because that's the best way of recovering. I'm sure she'll get in touch with Nicholas in due course.'

'I'm surprised he hasn't tried to get in touch with her himself.'

'Well, here's the thing—she's changed her mobile-phone number.'

'More pearls of wise advice from you?'

Lizzy shifted uncomfortably because his voice was mild and non-judgemental.

'No matter,' Louis continued, watching the shifting play of embarrassed colour shadow her face. 'You're trying to protect your sister and I can understand that. When I first went to Crossfeld, part of my brief there was to try and protect Nicholas.'

'You're being nice to me. Why?'

'Why shouldn't I be? We were very intimate, after all,' he was driven to include.

Lizzy cleared her throat and attempted to greet that aside in a businesslike fashion.

'I also should tell you that I have every intention of honouring my decision to make a contribution to your school.' He leaned forward and rested his elbows on his thighs, steepling his fingers and looking at her seriously over the tips of them. 'I liked what I saw.'

On safer ground, Lizzy allowed herself a small smile. 'That's not what some of the teachers say. We try and do at least three fundraisers every year—one at Easter, one at Christmas and one just before the summer holidays—but there's a limit to how much money we can make.'

She had a vivid memory of him in the playground, herding the little kids together so that he could involve them all in whatever game he had thought up on the spot. Yet again, her blinkered stereotype splintered to reveal an unsettling three-dimensional man who defied the categories she was so keen to put him into. 'The parents can only afford so much and no more.'

'And yet there's still an upbeat spirit amongst the teachers.'

'You noticed that, did you?'

'I notice everything. In big business, it pays to do so.' His dark eyes settled on her face, making her hot and flustered, although just at the moment there was no way that she could somehow pick an argument as a means for riding over the disturbing sensation. She hated thinking that he had found it so easy to walk away from her, but he was being so decent, and so damned uncharacteristically *generous*, that she couldn't possibly be anything but impressed.

'I've made an appointment with your principal, but I'll want you to show me around the school.'

'I'm not sure. Anita might want someone more senior to show you around the school.'

'I'm the potential benefactor. I get to choose.'

Lizzy felt a tingle of delight race up her spine but there was no way that she was going to allow him to see what was a very human reaction, all things considered.

'Now…' He drew her in to the conversation, his voice soft and persuasive. 'Tell me what sort of things I should be looking out for. But first, does this place do food? No? Probably better if I move my car, anyway. I know a cheap and cheerful Italian in Chelsea.'

'Cheap and cheerful?'

'Cheerful.' While she was still considering the option, and trying to work out how they were now communicating in this perfectly harmless manner, Louis engineered a fluid exit to his car.

Maybe this was what was needed, she thought. Just a bit of perspective. Maybe the perspective would take away that scary hold he seemed to have over her, bring him down a couple of pegs to the level of ordinary—or ordinary-ish, at any rate. And she *had* to go with him, didn't she? He was on the brink of donating vitally needed money to the school; he was calling the shots. Dinner at a cheerful though expensive place in Chelsea didn't seem like such a dangerous idea.

He kept her talking all the way to the restaurant, unthreatening, impersonal conversation about school policies and procedures, turnover rate of the kids, the quota of non-English-speaking pupils, the availability of computers. She asked him about the school he had gone to, a school she had heard of but never seen first-hand, and she found that she was listening intently to every word he said, thirsty for stray titbits of information about him.

By the time they made it to the restaurant, it was a struggle to remember the cause of her antagonism towards him. But she recalled it briefly and half-heartedly as they sat down at a table which seemed to have miraculously vacated purely for their convenience.

'I'm on personal terms with the owner,' Louis said by way of explanation, because the restaurant was packed to the rafters with people being turned away at the door.

Lizzy dimly remembered that they were poles apart, which was significant, although she couldn't muster the energy to let that bother her. She was tired, she was hungry and she had been thrown by his unexpected appearance at her place of work.

'Handy.'

'Are you going to give me a long lecture about the privileges that money can buy?'

But he was grinning at her and she smiled weakly back at him.

'I'm tired after a hard day at work, so can we just take it as read that I have?'

Louis laughed and looked at her appreciatively. More than

any other woman he had ever known, not only was she stubborn, outspoken and totally unimpressed by him, but she also had a sense of humour that could make him laugh out loud. That in itself was a first. Suitable women from suitable backgrounds, those women who fitted the category of potential marriage partners—if and when that time came—might be the safe option but since when had they ever been noted for their keen sense of humour? How perfect was his *perfect criteria*, really? Only perfect on paper. Lizzy Sharp broke all the rules.

'Deal,' he said, inclining his head to one side.

'And I'm only here because of the school-donation business.'

'Of course.' He watched as her mobile phone rang and she began rummaging in her capacious sack of a bag in search of it, muttering and cursing softly under her breath; he kept his eyes on her as he ordered a bottle of wine. He felt a twinge of intense curiosity as she turned away, huddling over the mobile and speaking quickly and quietly. Who was she talking to? What was with all the secrecy? And didn't she know that it was extremely rude to conduct long, involved conversations on a mobile phone whilst in the company of someone else? He conveniently forgot the many times he had done just that whilst out to dinner with one of his women.

But when she eventually finished the call it wasn't to apologise for her lapse in manners. Her face was drained of colour and she looked at him in silence for a few seconds.

'It's Leigh,' she said shakily. 'She's quit university and run off with Freddy.'

'*What?*'

'That was Dad on the phone. They don't even know where she is because they picked up the message on the answer machine. I think she might have gone into temporary hiding. Thing is, Dad said that they had heard rumours about Freddy being on drugs and they're worried sick.'

'He's been clean for years!' Louis growled. He raked restless fingers through his hair.

'I have to go!'

'Go *where*, Lizzy?'

'Back home.' She looked at him helplessly.

'You won't achieve anything if you go back to Scotland. You'll just ratchet up the anxiety levels. Freddy hasn't touched drugs since he was put into rehab, so that will be one worry off your parents' minds.'

'I know them. They've always worried about Maisie and Leigh. This will be their worst-case scenario. Not even Maisie knows where Leigh is, but she thinks that they might have gone and got themselves hitched. She's known him for all of five seconds! Literally. I know what you think of my parents, but you have no idea how worried they'll be. This will be the death of my father, on top of everything else.'

Louis reached out and took her hand firmly in his, and she let him. Her skin felt clammy.

'I'll find them.'

'How do you even know for sure that he isn't back on whatever he was on before he went into rehab? How? Leigh's never done drugs but she's pretty wild.'

'I know. And it'll be okay. You have to trust me.'

CHAPTER EIGHT

LIZZY didn't know how life could just carry on as though nothing had happened, but over the next two days it struck her that that was exactly what was happening. When Louis had held her hand in that restaurant and told her that everything was going to be okay, he had meant it. And she had trusted him.

He had delivered her home from the restaurant, having made her eat, and repeated at least a hundred times that Freddy might be shiftless, lazy and opportunistic but wasn't a junkie.

'And who knows?' he had mused. 'He's always made a point to target women who had money, and yet here he is, clearly besotted with one who hasn't a bean to her name. How the times are changing...'

Now, when her mobile rang and his name flashed up, she didn't hesitate to pick up. He had already called several times in the space of two days to find how she was, even though she assured him that she wasn't an invalid and, having put things into perspective, wasn't going to take on the problems of her family.

'Of course you will,' he had said, not hesitating to contradict her. 'It's your nature.'

Actually, Louis was enjoying the moment. Lizzy was the damsel in distress—a fictional character he had always considered vastly overrated—and he was the knight in shining armour, yet another stereotype he had never had much time for. And yet...

Sitting at his desk, about to collate information for a meeting, his mobile phone buzzed and with a slashing smile of satisfaction he picked up the call from her. Somehow, he had assumed the responsibility of always being the one to phone. It felt good to be on the receiving end of her phone call for a change.

'Lizzy.'

'Am I disturbing you?'

Louis shoved his chair back and swivelled it so that he was facing the broad expanse of window which, six floors up, offered a view of the sky and the tops of other buildings in the square mile. 'Not at all.'

'Look, I'm just calling to say, well, thanks for...you know. Phoning my parents. I guess they probably gave you a hard time.'

'Hold that thought. Where are you?'

'At school. No playground duty today, thank heavens. I was just about to leave, actually. Some of the others are going to the pub for a quick drink and I thought I might tag along with them.'

'What's the name of the pub?'

'Why?'

'I can be with you in forty-five minutes.'

'There's no need...' But a heady warm glow filled her, and she smiled as she paused in the staff room to gather her bag. Several of her friends were nudging each other and winking.

'If I had a pound for every time you said that.'

'You're already a rich man.'

Louis laughed; his meeting would have to wait. He had a sudden thought. 'Actually, why don't you come over to my place? I can order in some food for us.'

'Your place?' Lizzy licked her lips nervously. He had been

nothing but the perfect gentleman during this whole sorry business—more, in fact. He had comforted her, set her mind at rest and won her trust, despite all her initial misgivings. Why did she suddenly feel so scared at the thought of being in his apartment alone with him? Was she really egotistical enough to imagine that he would suddenly try to make a pass at her? She had warned him off and he had duly retreated. Sure, she had been a little piqued at his rapid surrender, but he had been there from the second she had received that distressing phone call from her father, and she knew that he was working behind the scenes, trying to locate the still missing pair.

'My place,' Louis said drily. 'It's slightly more comfortable than sitting in a pub.'

'Well…'

'My driver will be there to collect you in half an hour—and don't worry; you'll be dropped back to your place in one piece at the end of the evening. I may have some news for you, better delivered face to face.'

As trump cards went, that was the ace in the pack. Fifteen minutes later, having foolishly felt the need to wash her face and apply some make-up, Lizzy was sitting in the pub, cradling a glass of orange juice and eyeing the door with a mixture of trepidation and simmering excitement.

Every arrival set her heart racing, although when his driver did appear she knew instantly who it was because his neatly creased trousers and smart jacket, combined with his searching expression, screamed his identity.

Her heart didn't stop racing until they were in front of the imposing Georgian edifice at the very heart of one of London's most expensive postcodes.

Suddenly her casual clothes and flat shoes, the practical uniform she reserved for school, seemed horrendously inappropriate. When she reached to let her hair out of its braid, her hand stilled and she told herself that she was not in the habit of proving herself to anyone, and she wasn't about to start now. Least of all to Louis Jumeau.

Her sense of bravado lasted just about as long as it took the lift to ferry her from the gracious foyer, complete with the requisite security-guard sitting behind a grand marble desk, up to the top floor where Louis occupied a penthouse apartment.

He was waiting for her. He opened the door on the first ring and stepped aside. Lizzy paused and looked around her.

'Wow.'

'Can I take your coat?'

Lizzy stepped out of her coat and ventured into the vast open-plan area which cool marble expanse was broken only by a series of rugs that looked as though they must have cost the earth. To the left, a long, uncluttered island separated the kitchen from the living area. It was the sort of arrangement that could have only possibly worked for a bachelor who spent precious little time actually producing anything in his kitchen. Cluttered counters with practical gadgets would have ruined the clean, streamlined effect. The living area was as spectacular and as modern as everywhere else, with low, cream-leather sofas, and on the walls instantly recognisable abstract-paintings. Surprisingly, instead of the flat being contained on one floor, a staircase swept up to a galleried landing; she assumed that the bedrooms were upstairs.

All told, it was the most amazing place she had ever stepped foot into in her entire life, and she gradually became aware that her eyes were probably popping out of their sockets.

'This is a fantastic place.' She took a few steps forward and hoped that she wasn't leaving behind any tell-tale scuff marks from her shoes.

Louis looked around him, then back at her. 'I wouldn't have thought that it was exactly your style.'

'Well, no. I don't suppose I would actually enjoy living here, but it's still fantastic. Very grand.'

'I'm not sure whether to take that as an insult or a compliment.'

Lizzy blushed and finally looked at him. 'I'm sorry. I didn't mean to be rude, and thank you for sending your driver for me. It really wasn't necessary.' He was heading towards the kitchen and she followed him. 'Do you actually cook anything here?' she asked curiously. 'I don't think I've ever seen such a clean kitchen outside of a showroom.'

From behind the open fridge door, Louis glanced back at her and grinned. 'There you go again.'

It was that grin. The grin and the way he had rolled the sleeves of his work shirt to the elbows and undone the top buttons so that she could see the shadow of dark chest-hair. Her mouth went dry and she cleared her throat.

'And, yes, I do happen to cook here. Occasionally.'

'Real meals?'

'Qualify that.'

'Hot meals. The sort that most people might have for their dinner.' She accepted a glass of white wine that was ice-cold.

'I don't make a habit of it,' Louis admitted, indicating with a nod of his head that they should move into the sitting area.

Lizzy, busily taking her lead from him, decided that there was no need for her to remove her shoes, as he hadn't removed his. In fact, he didn't seem to care one way or another that she was grubby after a day at school and a hazard to his pristine furnishings.

'You can't eat out *every* night, surely?' Curiosity about him overrode interest in the goings-on of Leigh, Freddy and the rest of her family. In fact, it overrode everything else on her mind. She was dimly aware of a gnawing desire to prolong time in his company. How had she found the strength to see her mobile phone ring, knowing that it was him, and still resist the temptation to answer it? *Where* had she found the strength?

She felt overwhelmed. He was looking at her in a slumberous, sexy way that made her skin tingle. Did he know that he was doing that? Or was it just his way?

'You've got to understand that I'm out of the country a fair amount of the time,'

'But what do you do when you're *in* the country?'

'Should I be flattered at all this interest in my life?' Louis asked with rich amusement and Lizzy tried and failed to look polite but indifferent.

'I'm a teacher,' she said, thinking quickly on her feet. 'I'm programmed to be interested in other people. It's important to be curious about the kids, because not all of them have such great family backgrounds, and it pays to know what's going on on the home front.'

'Ah.' Louis crossed his legs and relaxed back as he looked at her thoughtfully over the rim of his glass. 'So this is all a natural-transference thing.'

'That's right.'

'In that case you'll be disappointed but maybe not surprised to know that I have a caterer who will happily stock my freezer with gourmet meals whenever I need them. I shove them in the oven and, hey presto!'

But this wasn't why she was here. There were important things to discuss and Lizzy wondered why she was beating around the bush. Was her curiosity about this man so intense? Why did she feel so weak and helpless the minute she was in his presence? It wasn't simply because she was attracted to him. This was much more than lust. At least, for her.

A dull pain throbbed at the back of her head as thoughts formed and took shape, like shadowy figures emerging from some dark place.

The memory of how she had felt deep down inside when they had made love leapt out at her, demanding to be analysed.

His eyes were fixed on her face and Lizzy felt the slow crawl of realisation begin to wash over her. He had made her feel wonderful. He had changed something fundamental inside her and there was no use pretending to the contrary. Against all common sense, against everything her head had told her she had managed to fall in love with him. All the prejudices she had pulled out of the bag hadn't been enough to stop the slide.

Elizabeth Samantha Sharp—outspoken, argumentative, contemptuous of women who would put their lives on hold for the sake of some guy—had done the unthinkable.

And the guy didn't even consider her worthy of a relationship! He liked the novelty of her, and was interested in her as a brief sexual partner, but that was about the sum of it.

Mortification brought a bloom of heated colour to her cheeks and she tore her eyes away from his sinfully handsome face.

'Okay. I didn't come here to have a long chat about *you*,' she said with spirit. 'You said that you had something to tell me about the whole situation, so it'll probably be best if you just say what you have to say and I can be on my way.'

'That wasn't the arrangement,' Louis said mildly, which made her frown.

'What are you talking about?'

'The arrangement was that we come here and I get some food in.'

Vulnerable and defensive, Lizzy eyed him with a superior expression. 'Do you mean to tell me that you're willing to get your pristine kitchen dirty by putting *food* on the counters?' Her lips twitched and she stifled nervous laughter.

'Yes, I'm about to consider the unthinkable and do just that.'

'But will you know how to do the washing up when we're finished eating?'

'No, wench. That's why you're here.'

Lizzy laughed. She wanted to tell him not to tease her, or to look at her the way he was looking at her now, because it undermined all her hard-won common sense.

'Now, you have a choice,' Louis told her, strangely seduced by the mellow mood and in no desire to hurry it along. 'Indian, Chinese or something from the Savoy.'

'Please don't tell me that you just said that.'

'What? Chinese? Indian?'

'"From the Savoy". Real people don't order in from the *Savoy*.' *I'm in love with him... How is that possible? How has that happened?* Shouldn't her good judgement have made her immune? She had always been the level-headed one in the family. Maisie and Leigh were careless and wild, Vivian got lost in her good deeds and Rose was the incurable romantic— but she, Lizzy, had always had her life in order and her emotions under control. So how had this happened? 'Real people actually clatter about with pots and pans and cooking utensils. Do you even know where your pots and pans are kept? You probably don't even have any, and if you do I bet you haven't got a clue how to use any of them!'

'Is that a challenge?' Louis asked lazily. 'Because, if it is, you should know that I have never been able to resist a challenge.' He didn't want to get down to the business of discussing Leigh and Freddy, Nicholas and Rose, or her parents. Ever a man to focus on the relevant and get on with dealing with it, Louis now found himself in the unusual position of just wanting to live for the moment. And right now, the 'moment' was talking to the woman sitting opposite him, hands resting lightly on her thighs, amusement glinting in her dark eyes. When it came to challenges, forget the small matter of his culinary skills; Lizzy Sharp was the greatest challenge he had ever encountered.

'And I'd bet you have nothing in that kitchen that could go into making a meal,' Lizzy scoffed.

'Maybe not a hearty Irish stew, but I'm well equipped for

anything that requires champagne, wine, butter and…' Louis frowned. What exactly was in his fridge? When had he last been in it, anyway? 'Let's go shopping.'

'I beg your pardon?'

'Shopping. There's a delicatessen five minutes away. Now that you've thrown down the gauntlet, I'm keen to prove my cooking skills. We can discuss other more serious matters over dinner. I don't know about you, but I would quite like to unwind for a while.'

Lizzy opened her mouth to tell him that she didn't feel comfortable unwinding with him, that he was at the very top of her hit list. Had it not been for him, Leigh would never have met Freddy, would not now be causing her parents sleepless nights and Rose would still be enjoying life on cloud nine instead of spending her days working through boxes of tissues.

But the thought of sitting on one of those leather bar-stools in his kitchen, watching while he cooked for her, was so alluring that her mouth actually felt dry. And she wanted to do things with this man; she wanted to absorb every minute of him like a sponge.

'Grab your coat.'

'You can't just take charge,' she said weakly. 'And I haven't got all evening to spend here. I only came because you told me that you had something to say to me.'

'Yes. And now I'm telling you that I'm going to rise to the challenge and cook you a meal. When it comes to taking charge, you should know that I'm an expert in the field.'

'You don't have to prove anything to me.'

'No?' Louis held out her coat so that she could slip into it. 'Then why does it always feel that way? And why do I like it?'

His breath was warm against the nape of her neck and his voice was low and pensive, as though he was really talking to himself. Lizzy shivered involuntarily and stepped away because being so close to him affected her ability to breathe.

This all felt so dangerous, yet so inevitable, and as she brushed past him out of the front door she was struck yet again at how easily control of her own life had slipped through her careless fingers. She wondered where the mouthy girl on the motorbike had gone.

The delicatessen was as close as he had said and was stocked with the most exotic array of food Lizzy had ever seen, at prices that made her eyes water. She watched with interest as he randomly chucked things into his basket and after a while she couldn't resist asking, 'Do you know what you intend to cook exactly?' She looked up at him and experienced a drowning sensation as his brilliant black eyes locked on her with amusement.

'I like to wing it when it comes to this sort of thing.'

'I'm beginning to see that.'

Half an hour later, she was relaxing on one of the bar stools in his kitchen, in front of a glass of crisp, chilled wine, with a wooden bowl of cheese-savoury biscuits in front of her. She had kicked off her shoes and, yes, against all odds she felt totally relaxed. Was he deliberately going on a major charm-offensive? Probably not. But he was being charming, talking as he chopped things, reminiscing about places he had been and people he had met. He was funny, sharp and utterly enthralling.

The kitchen was no longer what it had been. The floor was littered with bits of vegetables that had escaped his watchful eye and a cavalier array of condiments cluttered the counter space. Several attempts to toss whatever he was stir-frying had ended in chaos but he seemed unaware of the mess created.

Maintaining the necessary distance was difficult, and several times Lizzy found herself staring intently down at her feet, trying hard not to laugh.

'So...' She looked at him as he eventually finished his impromptu meal and approached her with a tea towel slung casually over his shoulder and a triumphant smile on his face.

'I gather you're not really that familiar with the basics of cooking.'

'What do you mean?'

'Most of the ingredients seem to have ended up on the floor.'

Louis, in buoyant spirits, looked down at the floor and frowned. 'How did that stuff get there?' He shrugged and tossed her a careless smile.

'Rule one,' Lizzy informed him primly, 'is to make sure that you clean as you go. Or else it's just a matter of time before everything descends into chaos.'

'I'm very ordered in my chaos.' Louis topped up her glass and indicated the living room. 'And if you adjourn to the living room you can pretend the kitchen doesn't exist. Food's going to be at least another fifteen minutes.'

Lizzy wondered how many glasses of wine she had had. Her head felt a bit woozy and she was relieved when she made it to the long leather sofa. 'I've had too much to drink,' she complained.

'You've had three glasses.'

'And one at the pub before I was collected. I'm not accustomed to drinking.'

'Close your eyes and relax.'

'I can't fall asleep in your apartment.'

'I know. That would be truly shocking.' Louis had never had a woman nod off in his company, but he was amused when five minutes later her eyelids fluttered shut and her breathing softened. He felt guilty and intrusive to watch her as she dozed but watch her he did. He noted the way her head gently fell to one side, the way her hand, balled into a loose fist, found its way to under her chin; the way her features softened. In between he set about cleaning the kitchen, a tedious task which he condensed into under ten minutes. And his lovingly prepared meal...

It was worthy of the bin. Clearly he had a long way to go

when it came to honing his culinary skills, but the attempt to actually use some of the utensils in his kitchen had been interesting. It only struck him later, when he was carrying a slumbering Lizzy into his bedroom, that she was the first woman he had ever cooked for. Even when he had been at university, he had had the financial resources to eat out.

She turned a little as he laid her down on his king-sized bed, and when he began removing some of her clothes he wondered whether she would wake up and how she would react. But was there anything worse than falling asleep fully clothed?

And it was hardly as though he hadn't seen her body before. In fact, he had perfect recall of all of it—although as everything but her bra and pants amassed in a heap on the sofa by the window he still felt his breathing thicken at the glorious sight of her. With a groan of frustration, he gently covered her with the duvet and watched as she burrowed under it until she found the most comfortable position.

Then he pulled over a chair, fetched the novel he had begun months previously, and which he had enjoyed reading until work commitments had relegated it to the bottom of the drawer, and took up position next to where she lay sleeping.

Three hours later, he dropped the book onto the bedside table as she began to stir.

'Before you ask, you fell asleep.' Louis sat forward, arms loosely resting on his thighs. 'And, no, you didn't get a chance to sample my fantastic dinner.'

Lizzy groaned and tried to focus. 'How long have I been out of it?'

'A little over three hours.'

Another groan, this time more dismayed. 'I'm so sorry.' She rubbed her eyes. 'This has never happened before. Those glasses of wine must have acted on an empty stomach. I didn't get time today to grab any lunch, and I haven't been sleeping well since all this business happened. I'm sorry you went to the trouble of cooking a meal and I fell asleep on you.'

'There's no need to keep apologising. I sampled the food and I can assure you that you didn't miss anything.'

Lizzy shot him a nervous glance from under her lashes. She began to work out how she had managed to go from the leather sofa to lying comatose on a bed in… She looked around her and registered that this was no guest room. This was *his* room: huge; airy; a vast expanse of window with privacy secured by banks of wooden shutters, and a massive bed with chocolate-coloured linen that felt silky soft against her skin. Against her…

Lizzy tentatively lifted the duvet and peered down at her semi-clothed body, then she raised her eyes to his as her mouth fell open.

'Where are my clothes?' She cleared her throat and then followed his hand as he casually indicated the chair.

'I thought you would be more comfortable.'

For the first time she noticed the chair by the bed, the book on the ground, the jug of water and the glass by the side of the bed.

'Were you in here with me the whole time that I was asleep?'

'Is that a problem?' Louis heard an edge of defensiveness in his voice and realised that his immediate response to her question had been to justify his uncharacteristic behaviour.

'Okay…' She strung that one word out. She had fallen asleep on him and in return he had *taken care* of her. What did that mean? Wary of embarking on an analysis of the situation—because she knew that it would be too easy to twist conclusions in a way that favoured him—she instead clutched the duvet and forced herself to be as brisk as she could.

'If you don't mind, I'll get dressed now, and perhaps we can actually talk about what I came here to talk about in the first place.'

'You want me to leave the room?'

'Of course I do.'

'Because I won't be seeing anything I haven't already seen…' And wanted to see again. Like a complete loser, he was prepared to take her rejection of him on the chin and stage another battle for her interest. 'There's an *en suite* bathroom and fresh towels in the cupboard. Feel free to take a bath or a shower; you can rest assured that I won't intrude.'

By the time she finally emerged from his bedroom, he had made them both a sobering cup of coffee and was waiting for her on the leather sofa, idly staring into space and not moving a muscle as she tentatively took the chair facing him.

'Mum said that you telephoned her,' Lizzy began without preamble. 'I phoned you to thank you for that. I don't suppose she gave you such a good reception when she heard your voice…'

She had washed her hair and, unlike all the women he had ever known, appeared to have no qualms about the fact that it was still damp. Nor did she mind sitting in front of him with a freshly scrubbed face. He had to drag his eyes away from the enticing wholesomeness of her.

'She seemed to share the belief that it was exclusively my fault that Rose and Nicholas had broken up,' Louis said abruptly. 'I made you a cup of coffee. Next to you on the table.' He could almost smell the clean, pine scent of his shampoo in her hair.

'Yes, well, I'm afraid I did tell her that you might have had a hand in that.'

'I telephoned Nicholas and had a talk with him.'

'You did?'

'He had to return to London to sort out an accident at a building which he had personally surveyed six months ago. There was some notion that he might have had culpability, but as it turned out the person who had been injured had been an illegal squatter. There was no question but that the correct signs were in evidence, and the owner of the building had no idea that it had been broken into. At any rate, he left Scotland the second he received the news, and it all took much longer than he had anticipated because he wanted to make sure that the guy who had been injured was all right.'

Lizzy's heart softened. 'But Jessica…'

'Played fast and loose with the truth for her own reasons,' Louis said in a hard voice. 'But, as you know, that wasn't why I called your parents. I called them to reassure them about Freddy.'

'Yes. Mum sounded a lot less frantic when I last spoke to her.'

'Which was the intention. As an aside, however, you might want to know that Nicholas has managed to get through to your sister at last. It's transpired that Jessica had told him that she had had a heart-to-heart with Rose, who wanted to end the relationship but didn't know how. Nicholas being Nicholas, he thought that he would retreat and give her some space, so when he returned to England he threw himself into sorting out the problem with the squatter and lay low for a few days. I think he may have hoped that Rose might get in touch, but that didn't happen, because she was busy thinking that she had been dumped.'

'Why on earth would Jessica say stuff like that?'

'She had her own agenda.'

'And you were at the centre of it.'

Louis shrugged. Lizzy stiffened and looked at him with flushed cheeks. 'Why don't you just put the poor girl out of her misery and marry her? She fits the bill, after all…'

Louis watched her carefully, his antennae tuned to her subtle changes in mood. 'I'm beginning to think that fitting the bill isn't quite as important as I've made it out to be in the past.'

Lizzy was determined not to be distracted. She had fallen in love with him; she knew that if Rose and Nicholas married then Louis would be around in some form or other for a long time, whether she liked it or not. He was Nicholas's closest friend. Rose was her sister. Ergo, she would be destined to bump into Louis at every family gathering, at every significant party, and neither would she be spared gossip about what he was up to, what he was doing, who he was seeing.

A vision of herself turning into a shrivelled spinster jumped out at her with nightmarish clarity: unable to move on, and condemned to witness first-hand Louis finding a suitable bride with the right background and having lots of suitable children. He would be the constant spectre in the background, reminding her of her unwise decisions and foolish behaviour.

So when he murmured like that, about fitting the bill not being as important as he once thought, she couldn't afford to melt, not even a little bit.

'Really? Well, I guess that's your business, but she must care very much about you if she's willing to make mischief with everyone's life to get her own way. Did she think that you would like her more if Rose was out of the way?'

'She thought that with Rose out of the way the ground would be cleared for Nicholas to marry my sister,' Louis said shortly. 'And then her chances with me would be vastly increased. She was deluded—and believe me when I tell you that I've dragged her kicking and screaming out of that particular delusion.'

Lizzy had a pleasing vision of Jessica being dragged by her glossy blond locks out of a house called Delusion and summarily chucked into a street called Reality—which was such an uncharitable thought that she flushed guiltily.

'Well, I'm glad that Nicholas and Rose have patched things up,' she said with genuine, heartfelt emotion. 'And have you been able to find out anything about Freddy and Leigh?'

Louis stood up and paced the room restlessly before sitting back down, but this time on the low, square uber-modern wooden table in front of her.

'What?' Lizzy asked anxiously.

'Good news and bad news on that front, as I'm pretty sure you'll find out for yourself.'

'Bad news?'

'You have a habit of fixating on the worst-case scenario.'

'It's better than living in cloud cuckoo land!' Lizzy said tartly. If only he knew that she was in danger of taking up permanent residence there, given half a chance!

Louis smiled wryly at her. Her hair had dried and was a riotous, tumbling mass streaming over her shoulders and his fingers itched to feel their silky length.

'The good news is that I've managed to locate Freddy and your sister.'

'Where?'

'In Las Vegas.'

'*Las Vegas?*'

'Having a wild time as the newly married Mr and Mrs Freddy Dale.'

Lizzy held her head in her hands and groaned. Her parents might have acknowledged that Leigh and Maisie were the wild ones in the family, but Leigh eloping and getting married— thereby depriving her society-conscious mother of the thrill of a fluffy white wedding—would hit them hard. Even if they would never have been able to stretch to the fluffy white wedding.

'I've made sure that they're booked on the next flight back.'

'How on earth did you manage to track them down?'

'Freddy is anything but cunning when it comes to spending money. He obviously withdrew a large sum of cash, but promptly ran out of money a couple of days into their adventure and was forced to use his credit card. As I told you, it's remarkably easy to track him down by following the trail of his spending.'

'I can't believe that Leigh could have been so *stupid*. I can't believe that anyone so clever could be so silly!' She cupped her face in her hands and peered up at him. 'Did you talk to either of them? Personally?'

'Much to Freddy's horror, I did,' Louis said drily. 'In fact, I spoke to *both* of them. It's always wise to get a second opinion when it comes to Freddy and what his side of the story is.'

'And...?'

'And it's all been sorted.' Louis allowed himself a small smile of satisfaction at this. Everything had a solution, and this particular solution had come to him in a heartbeat, although it went against the stance he had always taken with Freddy. Not only had he bailed him out, but the engine was now turning to do rather more than hand him out pocket money as he saw fit. For the first time, he was doing the one thing he had resolutely refused to do over the years—he was handing Freddy his independence. And he felt pretty okay about that.

He also knew that his solution could only meet with approval from the woman sitting opposite him and he felt pretty okay about that as well.

It was a win-win situation.

'What does *that* mean?' But that sneaking, treacherous inclination to rely on him was creeping over her.

'They want to set up a boutique-hotel halfway between here and Edinburgh, tailored to work hand-in-hand with Crossfeld—offering package holidays and complimentary golf at Crossfeld without the high prices, and also excursions into the city et cetera. Your sister's degree in tourism and marketing should come in handy, but I've told her that there's nothing doing unless she finishes her degree. It'll be tough going for a while, but I have people who can hold their hands until it kicks off. And Freddy... He's besotted with your sister and, reading between the lines, she doesn't sound the kind of girl who will let him have any leeway. He needs a woman to keep him in check. I think he's found one.'

'Hold on. This is just going way too fast for me.'

'Which bit of it?'

'The bit where I try and figure out how the blissful, newly wedded couple go from young and broke to opening a boutique hotel.'

'I am personally delegating sufficient funds to Freddy to enable him to set it up.' Louis frowned because this was not the unquestioning relief and gratitude he had expected. But since when had Lizzy Sharp ever done the predictable? Still…

'You mean you're *giving* him money, and by extension giving my *sister* money?'

'Is that a problem?'

'After everything you said about my family? After the accusations you've thrown at them? How can you expect otherwise?'

CHAPTER NINE

LOUIS threw up his hands in a gesture of exasperation. 'What ever happened to the graceful art of just saying *thank you*?'

Lizzy, intent on building fortifications around herself, and eager to cling to any excuse to impose distance between them, looked at him sheepishly from under her lashes.

He had taken time out to allay her parents' fears about Freddy and his reputation. He had taken time out to phone Nicholas and extricate the real story of what had happened, even though there must have been a part of him that was glad of the outcome of the misunderstandings, however deviously it had been made to come to pass. He had from all accounts dismissed Jessica, proving that, whatever he thought about the suitability of marriage between social equals, he still had his own standards. He had found Leigh and Freddy.

There was no necessity for him to have done that, just as there had been no necessity for him to have intervened in any of the myriad situations that had afflicted the Sharp family. And, not only had he intervened with Freddy, he had set him up with a means to a livelihood that included her sister, his wife after a whirlwind romance that could probably be entered into the Guinness Book of Records as the shortest in history.

It was no wonder that he was staring at her now as though she was something strange from another planet.

A wave of pure mortification swept over her. Had love displaced all traces of common civility?

'You're right,' Lizzy said quietly. 'And I'm sorry. I can't thank you enough for everything you've done.'

Louis narrowed his eyes on her face. Strangely, her softly murmured and clearly sincere capitulation left him cold. It was too polite, too distant. He realised that he wanted neither of those things.

'Yes. I'm a miracle worker.'

'Do you really think that Leigh and Freddy have a chance of making a go of this marriage of theirs?'

'Who knows?' Louis shrugged and looked at her broodingly from under his lashes. 'Does my opinion matter?'

'You're going to be handing over a great deal of money to them.' Did his opinion matter? Yes, it did, more than he could imagine possible. She tried to seek refuge behind her hastily erected defences once again, but the quizzical, penetrating expression on his face left her flailing.

Lizzy ducked her head and didn't say anything.

'Maybe the time is right for Freddy to do whatever he has to do with an inheritance that has been restricted because I didn't trust him to know how to use it. Maybe I think your sister would use it more wisely than he would.'

'You don't even know Leigh. What if she turns out to be one of those gold-diggers you've spent so much time telling me about?'

'What if?'

'You wouldn't object?' She tried to inject scathing cynicism into her voice but instead the scathing cynicism bore a remarkable resemblance to genuine curiosity. 'I mean, she could have manoeuvred Freddy into a situation of…of marriage.'

'By kidnapping him and transporting him to Las Vegas, before getting him drunk and forcing him into the nearest Elvis chapel? And all this using a crystal ball so that she could predict my putting some money their way so that they could set up a business of their own…?'

'That's exactly what you would have thought not that long ago!' Lizzy told him with spirit. 'More or less.'

Without the obvious exaggeration, Louis grudgingly admitted to himself that she had a point. Life had been a hell of a lot more straightforward when he had been thinking in clichés.

'True,' he conceded with a wry smile.

'Don't tell me that you're agreeing with me?' Lizzy said uncertainly.

'I'm big enough Are you?'

'Am I what?' A vision of unchartered, dangerous territory loomed in front of her like an endless ocean, full of currents that led to places she couldn't imagine, and loaded with perils against which she had no suitable armour.

'Big enough to admit to mistakes.'

'What kind of mistakes?' Lizzy asked suspiciously. Louis looked away to stifle a grin, because this was the Lizzy that he knew: not the one who caved in but the one who stubbornly stood firm in the face of whatever disapproving winds happened to be blowing in her direction. This was the Lizzy astride the way-too-powerful motorcycle, telling him exactly what she thought of him, never mind who he was, how much he earned, how many valuable paintings hung on his walls or how many houses he happened to own dotted all over the globe.

'I want to hear you admit that I'm not the bad guy you thought I was,' he encouraged her, enjoying the flame of colour that spread across her cheeks.

She made an inarticulate sound and looked at him with lofty superiority which, judging from his expression, he wasn't buying.

'You labelled me a snob.'

'You *are* a snob. Just look at your apartment!'

'Admit it, Lizzy.'

'Okay, so you're not all bad, I guess. I suppose.'

'And that would be because…?'

Lizzy glared at him but her heart wasn't in it. Really, her stomach was doing strange, flippy things and her eyes were all over him even though they didn't want to be. Even though they really should be focusing on anything but that beautiful face of his, and that body that was as lean, as powerful and as muscular as the most highly trained and toned athlete.

'I've already said thank you for everything you've done on behalf of Rose and Nicholas, and Leigh and Freddy,' she told him primly. But there was something in the atmosphere between them that was sending shivers through her, making her acutely aware of his proximity.

The silence that greeted this remark thrummed between them like a live electric current.

'You're looking at me,' she said in a choked voice. 'Don't look at me.'

'Why shouldn't I look at you?'

'I don't know what else you want me to say.'

'Of course you do.' Seemingly of its own volition, his hand reached out to brush the side of her face and Lizzy's breath caught painfully in her throat.

This might be just a simple gesture to him, but she was in love with him, and simple gestures like that became buried deep inside her like unexploded mines, waiting to detonate at some point in time when she would least expect it. She just couldn't give in. But neither could she seem to resist.

Her eyelids fluttered and she sat on her hands.

'You seem to have had an effect on me,' Louis murmured, half to himself, in such a soft voice that she had to strain with every ounce of her being to hear what he had said.

'What kind of effect?'

'You were right when you said that only a short time ago I would have suspected your sister of manoeuvring Freddy into a situation with the hope of money coming his way. You were right when you thought that I would have made no attempt to reconcile Nicholas and your sister because I had approached that relationship with the preconceived idea that she was on the lookout for a man with money. But that was then and this is now. I want you, Lizzy Sharp, and I want you to admit that it's mutual.'

Lizzy chewed her lip. The word 'want' sent an icy shiver down her spine. But the word 'regret' was even more scary. Making love to him that first time had been the most wonderful experience in her very inexperienced world, and to walk away from the opportunity of making love to him again was scary. A rush of wild, restless energy raced through her. She didn't want to think or work out the rights and wrongs of the situation, she just wanted to leap in, eyes wide open, and take whatever she could while it was there. Was that a sin? More than Rose and Leigh, she knew the rules of the game; however much he claimed to have changed, his change wouldn't run that deep, not when it came to his own personal life.

'Is that why you helped me?' she asked on a whisper. 'Because you wanted to get into my good graces so that I would agree to climb into bed with you?'

There was just the shadow of hesitation before he strenuously denied any such thing, just sufficient pause for her to know the answer to her question.

She squeezed her eyes tightly shut and pulled him to her. 'Okay. You win. I want you and I want you to make love to me, no strings attached.'

For Louis, 'no strings attached' should have brought a smile of triumph to his lips, but instead he felt a stirring of dissatisfaction. But the sweet smell of her was overpowering and, in one easy, fluid movement, he lifted her from the chair and carried her towards his bedroom while she clung to him with her hands clasped around his neck and her eyes closed.

The bed was still rumpled from where she had been

sleeping on it only a short while before. 'Open your eyes,' he commanded, moving to close the shutters and then switching on the Tiffany lamp on the chest of drawers so that a riot of light and shadow broke through the darkness in the bedroom. 'I want you to look at me. I don't want you to act as though this is just something that's happening to you. I want you to dive in and feel and see *everything*...'

He got rid of his shirt, tossing it on the floor, and then he pulled his belt through the loops of his trousers while he walked towards her. 'I could tie you up,' he said, dangling the belt from one finger and then laughing at her shocked expression. 'Maybe we'll leave that experience for another time...'

Lizzy's entire nervous system quickened at the prospect of that. The thought of being tied up by Louis Jumeau, at the mercy of whatever he wanted to do to her willing body, carried the thrill of the forbidden. And, while her body responded to those images in her head, her mind played with that throwaway remark: *another time...*

When he had disposed of all his clothing, he moved to stand directly in front of her, proudly and impressively naked. The ache between her thighs became ever more insistent as he curled his fingers into her hair and guided her to his erection. She felt his sharp intake of breath as her mouth curved around it and she began caressing it, using her mouth and her hands, touching him everywhere and loving the way his body was responding.

When she angled her body so that she could raise her eyes to his face, she saw that his head was flung back. The rise and fall of his broad chest sent a surge of heat pouring through her, pooling between her legs until she was aching to be touched.

Just then he looked down at her. His black eyes were hot and slumberous.

'I like watching you do that,' he said gruffly. He gently eased her off him and slid into bed with her. 'Your turn. I want you to undress very, very slowly. I don't want to miss a thing.'

Lizzy blushed and laughed under her breath, but she was already so turned on that taking off her clothes while he watched—propped up on one elbow, getting her to twist this way and that as each item of clothing fell to the floor—filled her with a heady wantonness.

She sashayed towards him when he crooked his finger and when he parted her legs with his hand she obeyed instinctively, her whole body trembling as he brought her towards him and positioned her so that he could taste her. She felt the exploratory push of his tongue as it slid along the moist cleft between her legs and she was panting as he complemented the action with his fingers so that she was bombarded with sensations that made it almost painful for her to breathe.

Her body was on fire when she eventually joined him on the bed, and she squirmed and writhed as he paid attention to her breasts, caressing them with his hands and licking her stiffened nipples until she wanted to scream.

Was it because she now recognised her love for him that made the experience so much *more*? She couldn't get close enough to him, and this time when their bodies could take no more he was prepared, reaching over to the drawer of his bedside table, taking care of contraception. This was, of course, incredibly responsible but it still made her feel cheap in some way—and she knew why. She would have loved nothing more than to conceive his child.

How awful was that?

If he could read her mind, she was sure that he would run screaming to the hills.

But he couldn't, and just in case those sharp eyes of his picked up any unconscious messages in her eyes she kept them lightly closed, grinding against his hard body. Then she wrapped her legs around his waist as he thrust into her and began moving in a rhythm that made her body sing in immediate response.

She couldn't understand how it was that he could be so damned good without having feelings for her, knowing just when to slacken his pace and when to pick it up. But then he was a male; making love was easy business for them. It wasn't an emotional rollercoaster-ride mired in all sorts of tangled feelings.

He might seem to know her body with the intimacy of someone who cared, but he was an expert. Other women probably thought exactly the same as she was thinking now when he started touching them. She wondered how many had fallen in love with him—even when he had played his noble trump-card and told them that he wasn't in it for the long haul, thereby leaving his conscience crystal-clear for when he disappeared over the horizon. Had Jessica fallen in love with him and then actually thought that he might commit to her because of their familial ties, because he happened to be her brother's closest friend?

'What's going through your head?' Louis asked, facing her on his side, and stroked some of her hair away from her face. 'I like the way you don't wear make-up.'

'You like the novelty of me.' Lizzy gathered herself sufficiently to face him and smile.

Louis wasn't sure whether he cared for that, but he was too damned content just at the moment to question it. And, anyway, she probably had a point. Everything about her was refreshing, and it wasn't just the fact that she wore no make-up. He found that he wanted to do things for her, unprompted and often without much hope of gratitude. It was strange but it was invigorating, and he supposed you could have called that the attraction of novelty. He just hadn't realised that his pallet had become so jaded.

'I come from a different class,' she said. 'Ordinary middle-class people who have spent their lives trying to achieve some financial security. Fat lot of good it did them in the end, with Dad and his crazy investments.' But that was something she would think about another time. It was just too big to take on along with everything else that had been going on in her life recently. 'I look different, I talk different and I work with underprivileged kids. I bet coming to my school was an eye-opener for you. I live in a completely different world to you. In fact, we might as well have been born on different planets.'

'Your sisters presumably all come from the same planet as you, but they're really not all that different from a lot of the women I've met in the course of my life—pretty, well groomed, wardrobes bursting with high-heeled shoes and small, black dresses.'

'What are you saying here?' Lizzy looked at him narrowly and tried to squash the heady feeling of delight his words gave her, because she knew that nothing he had said was intended to insult. He had looked below the surface and found things inside her that made her unique. Every optimistic cell in her body screamed for her to analyse that and come up with something promising.

'I'm saying that you break the mould.' He gave her a long, lazy smile. 'Like hearing that, do you? Are you going to return the compliment?'

'You break the mould for me, too,' Lizzy told him carefully. She wriggled as his hand swept along her thigh and rested on her waist while his fingers idly stroked her sensitised skin. 'But you know that. I mean, you're accustomed to luxury; you've had a life where money was never a problem.'

'That's the compliment?' His voice was light but it really wasn't what he wanted to hear.

'Well…' She stared at her fingers which were splayed across his chest and marvelled at the latent strength she could feel against them. 'It's the whole novelty thing.'

Louis frowned. 'The whole novelty thing?'

'You're my novelty, too. You're nothing at all like any of the other guys I've ever been out with.'

'Yes, yes, yes. I think we've covered this before.' Louis discovered that he had no interest in hearing about any of the other guys she'd been out with. In fact, he actively sought to discourage any such conversation.

'Okay. So…' She sat up, dragged the duvet to cover her and looked down at him. Gently he positioned her folded arms away from her breasts so that he could see her pink nipples peeping out at him.

'So…?' he murmured, already turning on for her again, and with such urgency that he couldn't possibly continue gazing at that brief glimpse of her breasts and had to reluctantly raise his eyes to hers. He lay back, folded his hands behind his head and looked at her. She looked loved-up. Her cheeks were rosy and her lips had the bee-stung look of a woman who's been thoroughly kissed. And, he thought with immense satisfaction, was going to be thoroughly kissed again. And again.

'So,' Lizzy continued in her best pragmatic voice. She had gone past the point of backing out of what they had. There was no room to start making excuses about being caught unawares, or making a mistake, and she didn't want to do either of those things. She loved him and she wanted him, and she was going to take what was on offer even if the odds against it lasting longer than a few months were high. She wasn't going to run from the prospect of a broken heart, because nursing a broken heart in the aftermath of what he gave her would be worth it. But neither was she going to turn herself into some kind of sex slave, with him calling the shots while she obeyed, doe-eyed and helpless. She might well be helpless, but she wasn't going to let him see that side of her. No way.

'So I think we should approach this in a businesslike way,' she carried on, clutching to this notion like a drowning man to a lifebelt.

'You're sounding like a teacher.'

'I *am* a teacher.'

'Not in the bedroom. When we're in the bedroom, consider our roles reversed. You get to play pupil. I like the thought of you responding to my every command.'

'I was saying…' Lizzy's voice was wobbly as she fought to get the conversation back on more stable ground. 'Point one, we've admitted that there's some sort of weird chemical reaction between us.'

'There you go with the teaching metaphors again.'

'And we *should* be able to fight it, because it doesn't make any sense. But point two, we're each other's novelty. So let's agree that we give this thing of ours a time limit. Say a couple of months? Get it out of our systems and then we can part company. How does that sound?'

'How does that *sound*?' Louis had never heard anything so outrageous in all his life. If mentally he had applied very similar guidelines to the relationships he had had in the past, he failed to make the connection now. He was frankly incensed that she would choose to destroy the ambience by dragging prosaic, unimportant and irrelevant technicalities into the equation.

And, more than that, he didn't like the thought of a time limit being put on what they had. Not at all.

For the first time in his life, he felt the pull to say the unthinkable, at least the unthinkable for the place he was in right now with his life. He wanted to submerge himself in this relationship and see where it went.

Acknowledging that felt as unsteady as peering over the side of a sheer precipice but, where he might usually have stepped back, he felt no inclination to do so—even if crashing over the side was the eventual consequence.

'How does that *sound*?' he grated, every muscle in his body rigid with tension. 'I've never heard such nonsense in my entire life!'

'But we've agreed—'

'*You've* reached your conclusions. Who says that I have to swallow them?'

'You're not a guy who commits to relationships, Louis.' She continued hastily, 'And we're not suitable candidates for a relationship anyway. At least, not any kind of relationship that matters. But we're attracted to one another.'

'Oh yes. The *chemical* thing.'

'So let's just face the limitations and be sensible about this.'

'And what if I don't want to face the limitations?'

'What are you talking about?'

'What if I think that this is too powerful for us to consign to a box labelled "controlled substance"?'

'This?' Hope flared like an explosion in her chest. The forbidden thought—that he might just have fallen in love with her despite all their differences and all the boundaries that existed between them—crept in like a thief in the night, temporarily doing away with all her caution, reason and sensible self-defence mechanisms.

'What we have going on between us,' he said with a sweeping, frustrated gesture. He scowled darkly at her and raked his fingers through his hair. 'I've never wanted a woman as much as I want you,' he admitted roughly. 'You're a first for me, and you make me behave in ways that I can't comprehend because they make no sense.'

Lizzy's mind was beginning to lag behind. Something about what he was saying didn't sit quite right. It came to her that he was talking about *wanting* her. Wanting her in the way someone might want a possession. Then she thought, what was the point in throwing caution to the winds if she became all tangled up in the detail?

'I want you, too,' she breathed huskily.

'Then let's not put restraints on this. Let's just see where it takes us.'

Sadly, Lizzy knew where it *wouldn't* take them: up the

aisle. But she wasn't going to refuse what was on offer. Her businesslike approach had made sense to her but, even if he had agreed, would she have been able to walk away at the end of the allotted time, had he asked her to stay on?

With a helpless whimper, she curved her body against his and slipped one leg in between his muscular thighs, nudging gently up, and laughing when he rolled her onto him so that there was no mistaking the evidence of his impressive arousal.

Her hair formed a long, unruly curtain around them and she pushed herself up so that her breasts could dangle provocatively close to his hungry mouth. She pretended to pull away, still laughing, watching as his eyes flared as he tried to catch one with his mouth. Each time her nipple brushed his lips, the ache between her legs became a little fiercer, until finally she had to succumb to the exquisite sensation of having him capture one pink nipple so that he could suckle on it.

It was a turn-on to look down at him from this angle and watch the movement of his dark head as he caressed her breasts with his mouth. For someone as controlled and as highly disciplined as he was, he made love with exuberance and a complete lack of inhibition. He might be able to guard his expressions when he wanted to, only reveal what he wanted the rest of the world to see, but naked and in bed he was a different man. Here and now, she could see the desire stamped on his face and feel it in the urgency of his touch.

She moved and, while he continued to attend to her swollen breasts, she eased him into her and then grinned as he looked up at her, his eyes dark and stormy.

'Don't stop,' she whispered. She began to move against him, long, slow movements; they continued to look at one another, she revelling in seeing him at her breast, and he enjoying the sight of her flushed cheeks and her fluttering eyelids as they began building towards their peak.

He placed his hands firmly on her buttocks. He only

stopped sucking her rosy, glistening nipples when he no longer
had a choice because he was going to explode.

They were damp with perspiration when Lizzy finally
subsided on top of him with a sigh of bliss, as sated and as
contented as the cat in full possession of the cream. His hand
was the icing on the cake, gently stroking her hair, and she
closed her eyes briefly and tried to imagine what it would be
like if he actually loved her; if this wasn't all about the good
sex.

'We're good together,' Louis told her thickly and she made
an inarticulate sound of agreement. 'Makes no sense, but there
it is. We're good together…' He pushed her a little, and reluctantly Lizzy rolled off him and then onto her side so that she
could look at him, although making love had made her drowsy
and all she wanted to do now was go to sleep. The night had
been so eventful that she was vaguely surprised that it still
seemed to be dark outside.

'Okay, I get that. We're good together—in bed. I agree.'

'It's not just about the sex,' Louis muttered, his eyes sliding
away from hers, and her heart gave a hopeful lift.

'It's not?'

'Of course it's not.' For a minute there, Louis had felt a
distinct lack of self-control but things were back in place now.
'You're clever, you're funny; it makes a refreshing change.'

'Oh, right. The novelty thing.' Disappointment flooded her
in a rush and she shoved it back.

Louis laughed and said something about a change being
as good as a rest. But when she failed to share the humour
he told her slowly and seriously, the idea coming to him out
of the blue, the result of some kind of effect she had on him.
'I've been thinking about the situation with your parents.'

He waited a few seconds for her to pick up on his cue, but
when instead she yawned widely and squirmed underneath the
duvet he laughed softly and kissed her shoulder. 'You're not

going to go to sleep on me for the second time this evening, are you?'

'I'm tired. I feel as though I've been through the wringer today. I've had more on my mind in the last couple of weeks than I've ever had before in my life. It's exhausting.'

'Then you can safely consider yourself free from future exhaustion.'

'What are you talking about?'

'I told you that I would take care of everything, didn't I?'

'And I told you that I was really grateful.'

'Except, I didn't quite take care of *everything*.'

'I can't think what you missed off the list.'

'Well, before you began falling asleep on me, I may have mentioned it—your parents.'

'Are doing fine, now that you've persuaded them that Leigh isn't going to become involved in some dreadful drugs-den with Freddy. In fact, when they find out about the marriage, and about your generosity in putting money behind Freddy's venture, they're going to be over the moon. Jobs are in short supply these days, and Leigh doesn't always come across as the ideal applicant for a position. It was just something else that was worrying them, so thank you for that. The down side, of course, is that Maisie will be losing her playmate. She and Leigh have been like twins all their life. It'll take some getting used to for Maisie now to have a married sister in charge of a business.'

'Not quite what I was referring to when I mentioned the situation with your parents.'

'No? What else is there to mention? Everything's fallen into place, like a jigsaw puzzle when the last piece has been put in.'

'Except for the small matter of your parents losing their house thanks to your father's unwise investments.'

'Ah. That. Well, on the bright side, at least there'll be no worry about Rose or Leigh—and, before you tell me that they're going to target Nicholas as some kind of private-banking system, they won't.'

'I wasn't going to tell you that. I was going to tell you that I've instructed my accountant to sort out their debt problem. They'll be able to keep the house. I'm going to give them the money.'

Lizzy froze. 'You're *what*?'

'I'm going to give them the money. I didn't mention this to you, but I had a pretty long conversation with your father about those investments he made. Yes, they were pretty stupid, but he'd run his affairs in a fairly tidy fashion up until then and I'm convinced that lessons have been learnt from this.'

'You've spoken to my father and told him *what*, exactly?'

'That I would see what I could do about recuperating some of the money he's lost. Naturally I didn't talk about a rescue package, but essentially I will ensure that there are no debts hanging over his head and no worries about losing the house they've lived in since they were first married.'

Lizzy felt cold, hot and cold in sickening waves. She pushed herself up and slipped her legs over the side of the bed and was aware of Louis moving around the bed to confront her.

With quick, shaky, frantic movements she dragged the duvet from the bed and wrapped it protectively around her nakedness.

'What the hell is going on?'

'There's no way that you're going to bail my parents out!'

'What's wrong with you? I thought you'd be pleased.'

Lizzy didn't dare look at him and she wished that he would just do the decent thing and put some clothes on. Ranting at a naked Greek god lookalike was so much more difficult.

'And look at me!' Louis roared in bewildered, enraged frustration.

'You throwing money at my parents, in a rescue package that's not a rescue package, makes me feel soiled!' she flung at him furiously. 'It makes me feel as though you're *buying* me.' She dodged past him and headed for her clothes strewn on the ground, although progress was severely impeded by the weight of the duvet.

'Work that one out for me.'

'Work it out for yourself!' She managed to grab her clothes, shed the cumbersome duvet and fly into the *en suite* bathroom in the space of five seconds. Once there, she locked the door behind her and leant against it, breathing heavily and steadying her nerves, which were shot. Any thought of a shower couldn't have been further from her mind and she just washed her face, making sure not to look in the mirror, and then stuck on her clothes before taking a deep breath. Louis, waiting outside, would be a towering inferno.

But thankfully a clothed one, although the clothing only consisted of a pair of black boxers. He was looming by the window, arms crossed, waiting.

'I thought that being attracted to you was enough,' Lizzy told him, making sure to keep a safe distance. 'But it's not.' *Because you still think that it's all about the money.* Instead of expensive gifts, he would give her parents bail-out money. 'You give my parents money, and for me that would be the equivalent of being bought—and do you really think that I have a price? Did you think that I would have to be forever grateful to you, and therefore you would have the right to enjoy me whenever you wanted?'

'I've never heard so much rubbish in my life!'

He made a move as though to get closer to her, and she stumbled back until she had her back to the bedroom door.

'In the end, it's all about money for you. What you can buy. *Who* you can buy.'

'Your parents were in financial difficulties; I am in a position to help them, and I wanted to because you're in my life.' He faltered to an awkward stop and half-turned away from her. 'You drive me crazy,' he muttered under his breath.

'You've done enough, and I don't want you giving anything to my parents. I have some savings. I can help out however I can.'

'Don't be ridiculous. You have no idea the extent of how big your father's debt has become over time.'

Lizzy pulled open the door and took a backward step out of the bedroom while she continued to watch him warily, the way someone might watch a tiger poised to attack. But he wasn't approaching her. Already she could feel him letting her go. She was too much trouble. Her heart felt as though it was literally cracking open, but the mantra playing in her head was *it's better for this to happen now.*

Maybe, subconsciously, she had fancied her chances at becoming indispensable to him; maybe her decision to take what was on offer had been more to do with that little seed of hope than a sudden, daring recklessness on her part. Who knew? But she knew now, and conclusively, that she would only ever be one in a line for him, maybe lasting a little bit longer because of her novelty value. He would have bought his expensive, well-groomed, well-manicured women diamonds and exotic weekends abroad—and her? Well, he would buy her her parents financial security because she wasn't the 'diamonds and exotic weekends abroad' type.

'I don't need to!' Was she being selfish? She had no idea just how far into debt her father had dug himself, but she guessed that her paltry savings weren't going to go a long way to curing the problem. For a few agonising seconds, she was gripped by indecision, but then she rallied. 'And I don't want to see you again. It doesn't matter how enjoyable this… this…' she waved her arms helplessly in a sweeping gesture '…*thing* we have is. It's just not enough.'

'You're overreacting.'

'Don't tell me that I'm overreacting!'

'When you calm down, you'll see that what I'm offering makes sense; if you feel better, I can construct it as a loan.'

Now he was lowering himself to accommodate her crazy mis-interpretation of the situation? Louis could scarcely credit it, and confusion rooted him to the spot.

But Lizzy was on a roll. What filled her mind was the repulsive notion that he was throwing money in her direction with the intention of buying her for however long he wanted. He had clumped her in with all those women whose beds he had shared, women who had been willing to accept gifts from him and disregard the fact that the greatest gift of all—his commitment—would never be on the agenda. And she couldn't even blame him! She had been as eager to hop in the sack with him as every other woman, so how could he expect her to react differently to his choice of present? Except his choice of present somehow made her feel soiled.

'I don't want you constructing it as *anything*,' she snapped in stubborn, blind refusal. 'Thank you for everything you've done, but now I just want you to step out of my life!'

'There's something going on here that I'm not getting,' Louis grated with menacing intent. 'What is it?'

That I'm in love with you, Lizzy thought bitterly. *Hence I would have given you anything you wanted—but the second you put money on the table it feels like an ugly trade-off...*

'I *wanted* to sleep with you,' she told him in a more sub-dued voice, picking over the truth and extracting the bits of it she could share. 'I was willing to finally admit the attraction between us and not run away from it. I *knew*,' she was com-pelled to stress, 'that we weren't suited on any level except the physical, but I was willing to overlook that. But your offer, your *kind and generous* offer to bail my parents out of their debts, felt like a down payment on my body, and I'm sorry but I can't deal with that. You are who you are; you can only think of people in terms of money—and please don't tell me that I'm being ridiculous.'

She drew in a deep breath and waited for his continuing fury but instead he half-turned away from her.

He said, over his shoulder, in the tone of someone voicing an afterthought, 'Fine. We gave it a shot; it didn't work. I'll make sure to avoid you whenever possible. If you leave details of your school's email address and anything else relevant I might need, I'll make sure my accountant deals with my donation. Unless, of course, you'd like to object to that as well. No? In that case, you know how to find your way out.'

CHAPTER TEN

HAVING caused enough stress and worry to last a lifetime, Leigh, now Mrs Dale, was keeping a low profile. Much to Maisie's disappointment, she no longer had her party buddy for whenever she returned home. But, six weeks after the story of the hasty marriage unravelled, Maisie had bounced back, although much to her parents' delight she was no longer in need of constant supervision. She had been sobered by Leigh's marriage and by the startling fact that Leigh seemed to be taking her new-found responsibilities seriously. Studies were back on with a vengeance, it seemed, and plans were enthusiastically afoot for finding premises for the new business venture.

Nicholas and Rose were ecstatically engaged and the church was booked. They were to tie the knot as soon as possible—so soon, indeed, that an engagement seemed a bit surplus to requirements. The hunt was therefore on for the perfect dress and, although Rose tried her hardest to involve Lizzy in the search, Lizzy couldn't summon up the necessary levels of energy for the project.

News and updates were being received via her mother or one of her sisters. Safely tucked away in London, she could involve herself, but only as far as she wanted, and there was no chance that any of them could ferret out her fragile state of mind from a disembodied voice down the end of a telephone.

So, while she languished miserably on the sofa in front of her television, with a stack of exercise books waiting to be marked and proving an ideal distraction, she listened to her mother tell her about Leigh and Freddy's first sheepish visit to the family house after they had returned from Las Vegas.

She exclaimed with appropriate delight at Nicholas's romantic marriage-proposal and the rather large diamond now sitting proudly on Rose's finger. She listened to Maisie whinge about Leigh growing up and getting boring, then awkwardly muse that she, too, was getting sick of the same old parties. She spoke to Rose virtually every other day and, whilst she was genuinely happy for her sister, she couldn't help wallowing in a certain amount of sadness and self-pity every time she listened to yet more arrangements being made for The Big Day.

It made her wonder how her life had managed to get so comprehensively derailed when she, out of all her sisters, had always been the most practical and level-headed. She hadn't breathed a word to anyone about Louis. She knew that, if she had chosen to tell Rose, her sister would have gently pointed out that she might have been too hasty, might have let her prejudices rule her and been too proud to look back.

Whenever Lizzy heard those imaginary conversations in her head, she reminded herself that Louis had behaved appallingly and that he had somehow tried to buy her.

Which didn't stop her wondering how he was and what he was doing. His image was so deeply seared into her consciousness that she couldn't get him out of her mind. Several times she fancied she spotted him striding in front of her, and she felt her heart begin to thud and her pulses begin to race, but it was never him.

She knew that he had made a massive donation to the school, and the principal was in a state of high excitement at the prospect of being able to get some really decent equipment into the classrooms and the outside playing area. The roof was going to be mended and there was even talk of a separate computer-block being built.

In fact, a special dinner was held for him in his honour, but she declined to go on the spurious grounds of not feeling very well. Just the thought of actually seeing him and hearing the sound of his voice brought her nervous system close to a state of meltdown.

Not that Lizzy expected to avoid him for ever. He would be at Rose and Nicholas's wedding, and there was no way that she could decline *that* invitation on the spurious grounds of not feeling very well.

But as the time drew closer her sense of dread increased. She would be heading back up to Scotland three days ahead of the actual ceremony so that she could help out. There was going to be a lavish reception at Crossfeld, the west wing of which was almost completely renovated thanks to wads of money being thrown at the refurbishment. Vivian would be returning home for a few weeks, and according to her mother would be returning with a guy, a fellow missionary she had met in Africa. It had occurred to Lizzy on more than one occasion that she might end up the last in her family to marry—if she ever did. Given how broken her heart felt at the moment, that didn't seem to be much of a possibility.

With spring approaching, the weather had lightened, and she arrived in Scotland on the Tuesday to what was an unusually brilliant day for that part of the world, with more to come, if the forecasters were to be believed.

And no sooner was she back in the family home than she was in the thick of it. Vivian filled her in on her travels and she met the boyfriend, Edward McGinty, who in a curious twist of fate was Scottish, had been to the same university as Vivian, although on a different course, and lived just outside Glasgow. He was pleasant and kind and seemed bewildered at the level of activity in the house. Her mother was all over the place, while her father sat it out in his shed at the bottom of the garden, tinkering with a coffee table he had been making for what seemed like years.

A newly focused Leigh grabbed every opportunity she could to describe her plans for the sparkly future ahead of her, and spent inordinate amounts of time on the telephone to Freddy, who had stayed behind to look over a couple of possible locations for their venture. Maisie drifted irritably from room to room, bemoaning the fact that peach was such a *passé* colour for the dresses, until Rose finally told her to shut up.

There were clothes everywhere, bridesmaids' dresses, which Lizzy was relieved to discover fitted her and needed no alterations. The bridal dress was hung in Rose's wardrobe under protective plastic, although she did try it on for Lizzy to see, and was oblivious to the shadow that crossed her sister's face underneath the admiring smile.

She heard mention of Louis so many times that by the time she retired in the evenings her head was literally throbbing. Unsurprisingly, he seemed to have become flavour of the month, or possibly even the year.

It was only on the eve of the wedding, when everyone had retired to bed for the requisite early night, that Lizzy had a chance to sit and chat to her dad. His appearances over the past few days had been brief, but now he was in the sitting room with his feet up quietly watching the television.

'Peace. At last.' He smiled at Lizzy and raised his eyebrows. 'Not heading upstairs for some beauty sleep? Not that you need it, pet; you're beautiful enough without it.'

'It's mad here.' She went to sit on the chair next to him and sighed. 'I bet you can't wait to get it all out of the way.'

'*I* can't, but you know your mother. She's in her element arranging everyone around her, and moaning that it was all too rushed to be perfect, although she seems pretty pleased with the outcome so far.'

'Dad, I really want to talk to you about your financial situation.' Should she mention Louis and his interference? No; she would pretend that none of that had happened. She didn't know the precise details of Louis's conversation all that time ago with her father. He could just have given some helpful advice without having promised any form of financial bailout. She would assume that.

She opened her mouth to launch into the chat she had had with her bank manager, but before she could get anywhere her father looked at her with a smile.

'You know that this must remain between us, pet...' He beamed. 'And I know that your friend Louis told me to keep this under my hat, but I'm sure he wouldn't mind you knowing that he's helped me out of a tight spot. A very tight spot indeed. Of course, it's on the basis of a loan, but we both realise that the chances of it being repaid in full are very slim indeed. And he did more than that, Lizzy. This whole bash is at his expense by way of a wedding present to the couple. He's a generous man, that one.'

Lizzy felt sick. 'When...when was all this sorted out, Dad?' she asked faintly. Yes, just as she had expected, it had all been sorted out weeks previously. She had struck out at him, told him that she never wanted to see him again, informed him that she wasn't interested in any donations to her family, and quietly he had gone behind her back and helped her father.

Why? He hadn't wanted her to be told. She listened to her father wax lyrical about Louis, while her stomach churned and a million unanswered questions sprang into her head and vanished before she could pin any of them down for examination.

Forty-five minutes later, she was virtually pushed out of the room and told to get some sleep. Everyone else in the house was asleep and he wanted to savour a glass of single-malt whisky on his own, because for the first time in a very long time indeed he felt on top of the world.

Lizzy duly fled, not wanting to risk another eulogy about Louis.

However, the following morning, her thoughts were all over the place. Cars had been hired for delivery to the church and then on to the grand reception at Crossfeld. She would be sitting in her long peach dress in a car paid for by the man with whom she was hopelessly in love and whom, she sickly feared, she had dismissed for reasons that had to do with her and not with him.

She observed her family in the detached manner of someone looking at events evolve from a distance. Rose, she noted, looked spectacular—radiant, happy and unbearably beautiful. Leigh was calmer than she ever had been, looking forward to seeing Freddy. Vivian was no longer as hectoring as she had been before she had gone to do her stint abroad. She was holding Edward's hand in the car, and Lizzy saw that love had invested a certain amount of tranquillity in her. Even Maisie, always the most hyper of the lot, was smiling and pleasantly subdued. None of them were having to cope with thoughts rampaging through their heads like an army of fire ants. No, that was *her* lot.

And because she had made a mistake—a series of mistakes. She had tried to shove Louis into a box, and when he hadn't fitted in snugly, she had proceeded to carry on with her misjudgements and preconceived misconceptions nevertheless. Instead of asking herself the fundamental question: if he had been so monstrously unacceptable, then how was it that she had managed to fall in love with him?

She was in a state of feverish excitement by the time the cars pulled into the wide gravelled courtyard outside the church.

Whatever the outcome, she would have to put things right or else how would she ever be able to live with herself?

The church in the early spring sunshine brought back a host of memories. It was the church her parents had always attended, and she could remember following in their wake as a child, sitting in the back pews with her sisters fidgeting next to her, trying to stifle her yawns. She had never appreciated how picturesque it was, with its background of rolling fields, and its warm, mellow stone, aged over many decades.

The little church was reduced to standing-room only and all heads swivelled as the organ heralded the arrival of the bride. Lizzy, walking behind Rose and her father, kept her eyes fixed firmly ahead of her but her fingers were clutching the bouquet of flowers as tightly as if she was on a white-knuckle ride.

As they neared the pulpit, Louis swam into focus, standing to one side, his eyes observing the procession dispassionately.

In his formal black suit, he looked drop-dead gorgeous, but when she tentatively looked at him it was to find him coolly stare back before looking away, not a flicker of emotion on his face. Doors had been very firmly shut, she thought miserably, and she had no one but herself to blame.

It took a great deal of will power to focus on the ceremony and to appreciate that it was her sister's day, and that whatever attention she had would have to be directed at Rose and Nicholas, rather than inwards onto her own frame of mind.

But it was hard, and she was relieved when it was over and Rose was stretching up to Nicholas with a blissful smile on her face, kissing him.

And then there was very little time to focus on Louis as photographs were taken, bouquets were tossed and people jumped into cars to begin the journey to Crossfeld. Louis, she noticed with a sickening lurch in her heart, was not travelling alone. A pretty brunette was with him, and together they climbed into a silver Maserati. Lizzy had to look away because she knew that, whilst she had been busy wallowing in her unhappiness, he had obviously picked up the reins of his life and got on with the business of moving forward.

It should have been enough to construct the foundations for feeling a sense of some self-justification, but it didn't, and she followed him anxiously with her eyes as Crossfeld House swelled with guests.

The brunette might not have been the sort of blonde bombshell she had expected, but there was a level of warmth and familiarity between them that made her want to run away and find a quiet spot somewhere so that she could take refuge from her unhappiness.

Only when the food had been served did she finally find the courage to seek him out, and it took some doing. Maybe he was a little fed up with being surrounded by so many people, because when she finally located him it was purely by accident and in a place she least expected, in a large room far from the crowds which appeared to be in the process of renovation. The walls had been stripped of wallpaper, the carpet had been pulled out and sheets of plastic covered the items of furniture. He had pulled off some of the plastic over a chair by the fireplace and was sprawled in it, his head resting back, his eyes closed.

He was holding a full glass in his hand but he looked done in, and Lizzy paused for a few seconds in the doorway before walking in without making a sound to announce her arrival so that she was literally standing over him when he finally sensed her presence.

'I know I'm probably the last person in the world you want to see now,' she began.

'What are you doing here?'

'I… I wanted to talk to you.'

'I'm done talking to you, Lizzy.' Louis stood up abruptly and she fell back, alarmed at the thought that he might just walk away from her and she'd be left with all these unspoken thoughts whirling around in her head, making her life a never-ending round of regret and self-recrimination.

On impulse she reached out and placed her hand on his arm; he paused to look down at her hand and then directly at her face.

'I'm… Please, Louis, can't you even hear me out? I'm sorry.'

'That it?'

'No. I don't like the way we left things the last time we spoke. Can we sit down, please? You're making me nervous.'

'I'm not sure why you think I care.'

'No, you don't; I know that. But *I* care.'

Louis stilled, then he gave a lazy shrug before strolling over to one of the sofas and yanking off its plastic covering. He sat down, crossed his legs and watched as she awkwardly perched alongside him.

'There's a wedding going on out there,' he drawled. 'So unless you have something new to say to me, why don't we skip the post mortem on what happened between us?'

A flash of anger stirred in her and she subdued it because she was not going to fall into the trap of reacting to his indifference.

'My father told me that you lent him the money. I know I gave you a long lecture about staying out of my family's financial problems but I feel I need to thank you.'

'I gave your father strict instructions to say nothing to you about that.'

'I know, and—'

'So you've said your piece. Thanked me for my generosity. Is that it?'

'Not quite.' In a split instant, Lizzy made her decision. 'I've missed you, Louis. I know you've carried on as though nothing happened of any consequence in your life, and I know that as far as you're concerned I was just a passing fling who turned out to be more trouble than she was worth, but you were more for me than a passing fling.'

It took so much courage to lay her cards on the table, especially when she thought of the brunette waiting back outside in the throng of guests—but if she didn't lay her cards on the table she had a sinking feeling that she would spend the rest of her life reshuffling the deck and filling her head with 'what ifs' and 'if onlys.'

She could feel his attention on her now one-hundred percent, although his face remained impassive. It was making her nervous and she looked away, staring down at her fingers worrying the fine peach silk of her dress.

'I didn't want to let myself give you the benefit of the doubt.' She quietly addressed her lap. 'It felt safer to think of you as an arrogant, selfish, snobbish cardboard-cutout. It felt safer to think that what I felt for you was just lust, because lust is something that disappears quickly. I didn't want to admit to myself that I was falling in love with you because I knew that loving you was never going to get me anywhere.

'And don't get me wrong—I'm not asking for any second chances, and I'm not saying that I'm going to jump into the sack with you. I'm saying that what you did for Dad was kind and generous. You might be guarded and suspicious about gold-diggers and money grabbers but you… Anyway, there you go; I've said what I wanted to say. I'm going to leave you now. I know you and your new girlfriend are probably going to have a good laugh about me behind my back, but I'm glad I've been honest with you.' She made a move to stand up and felt the weight of his fingers on her hand.

'What girlfriend?'

Still not daring to look at him, because she didn't want to see the pity in his eyes, Lizzy shrugged and muttered, 'The brunette you came here with.'

'I don't like it when you don't look at me—and the brunette you're referring to happens to be my sister.'

Lizzy looked at him then and began drowning in the depths of his fabulous eyes.

'Why didn't you come and tell me all of this sooner?'

'I thought I could handle things, but the past few weeks have been hellish.'

'I know.'

'*You* know?'

Louis's fingers were stroking the soft underside of her wrist and Lizzy could barely stop her heart from hammering furiously in her chest, beating out a tempo of hope and wishful thinking that terrified her.

'You turned my life on its head,' Louis said in a rough, uneven voice. 'I had my own blinkered vision of life, and bit by bit you broke down my prejudices until I was acting so out of character that I could hardly recognise myself.'

'What are you saying?' she whispered, perched on the very brink of daring to think the impossible.

'I *wanted* to help your father, just like I *wanted* to do whatever I could for your sisters, because of you.' He reached out and stroked the side of her face, her adorable, lovable, stubborn, wilful, absolutely irresistible face—the face that had haunted him for weeks and had interfered with every second of his waking life. 'I think I've been falling in love with you from the very second you took off that motorcycle helmet and gave me a piece of your mind. Why do you think I kept coming back for more? I just couldn't help myself. I went from the guy who had every inch of his life under control to the guy who no longer knew the meaning of the word.'

'You *fell in love* with me?'

'I fell in love with you, Lizzy Sharp, and I don't think I know how to stop falling.' He didn't have to pull her towards him because she came of her own accord, burrowing against him just as he had remembered her burrowing against him after they had made love. He curled his long fingers into her hair, pulling out the clips that had artfully held it up until its length spilled over his hands, just the way he liked it.

He felt her shudder against him, and when he tilted her face to his her eyes were half-closed and her mouth was ready to be kissed. And every other part of her was ready for his questing hands, turning her on through the soft fabric of the dress.

'Will you marry me?' he asked, breaking away to look at her flushed face. 'And I mean instantly, as soon as possible— no tedious engagement.'

'Instantly.' Lizzy was so happy that she wanted to cry. 'As soon as possible and no tedious engagement.'

'Good. Because you make my life complete, my darling. Without you, there's no point to anything. I fell in love with you and I'm no longer interested in having control of my life. I'm willingly handing it over to you…'

In any event, they waited until Rose and Nicholas had returned from their honeymoon before announcing their plans to family and friends. It was going to be a small affair. After the extravaganza of Rose's wedding, Grace Sharp was more than happy to oblige, although it had to be said that she was every bit as excited about something quiet and elegant.

'I know just the band who can play, and wouldn't it be a good idea if Leigh and Freddy handled all the catering? What an advertisement for their business once they're up and running!'

'At least I won't have to wear a peach gown when I'm far more comfortable in something small and sexy,' Maisie announced, laughing at Rose's disapproving face before adding slyly, 'and the way this family is dropping like flies, I wouldn't be a bit surprised if you or Leigh end up having to squeeze into something loose and flowing to cover the bump!'

Her father was over the moon, although he did sit and have a long chat with her, because as with all his daughters he needed to make sure that it was all about love.

'And my record is pretty good so far,' he told her comfortably. 'A dad couldn't wish for more.'

It was a mere three weeks between proposal and marriage, and not a day went by that Lizzy didn't feel adored by the one man in the world who meant everything to her. She had moved into his penthouse apartment, but they were already looking for something outside London, close enough for him to commute when he needed to, but distant enough to benefit from the country lanes and open fields she so missed.

'But the motorbike stays in Scotland,' he warned her, half-teasing, half-serious. 'I would become a nervous wreck if I thought about you haring down lanes on that thing.'

Lizzy was more than happy to oblige. If she had tamed him, then he had similarly tamed her.

Their wedding was small, quiet and absolutely perfect. Leigh and Freddy catered, and lest anyone might forget their role in the proceedings they liberally handed out their business cards to all and sundry. Maisie, as promised, wore something small and tight which seemed to have the desired effect on one particular guest, a friend of Louis. Vivian and Edward actually made the long-haul trip back because, she said fondly, 'We girls stick together.'

Three weeks after they had found the perfect new London residence for them both—not too grand, not too small—Lizzy cooked Louis a special supper, complete with candles and soft music. As always the sound of his key in the door and the sight of him walking through, tugging off his tie, made her tummy quiver. When he raised his eyebrows in a question, she laughed.

'Before you ask, I'm not in any danger of turning into a Stepford wife.'

'Good.' Louis walked towards her and pulled her to him so that he could kiss her, a long, lingering kiss which, as usual, made thoughts of bed spring into his head. 'Because...' He drew away and smiled down at her. 'I'm not sure I could cope with one of those.'

It was only when they had finished eating that she looked at him and said, unable to contain her news any longer, 'You might want to savour the time we have left together.'

'You mean here? In this apartment? Before we move?'

Lizzy qualified, dropping the air of mystery and beaming at him, 'Before you become a father—in, I would say, approximately seven months' time.'

It was the icing on the cake. For Louis, he had found the perfect woman, and a swell of pride and contentment filled him as he gathered her to him and held her tightly. The perfect woman, and soon a baby to complete a picture he had never known he had envisioned—until Lizzy Sharp had come along and shown him that there were no boundaries to love and no regulating the winding course it took you on.

TOO PROUD TO BE BOUGHT
by Sharon Kendrick

Experience has taught Russian oligarch Nikolai Komarov that all
women have their price, but he's never encountered anyone like
waitress Zara Evans—a young woman too *wilful* to be bought…

PRINCE OF SCANDAL
by Annie West

Prince Raul is furious when an archaic law forces him to marry
reluctant princess Luisa Hardwicke. But outspoken Luisa
challenges Raul at every turn—and he finds himself eagerly
anticipating their wedding night!

STRANGERS IN THE DESERT
by Lynn Raye Harris

Isabella, the wife Sheikh Adan thought was dead, has walked
back into his life—but gone is the dutiful, pure girl he once
knew! In her place is a defiant, sultry woman…who has no
memory of being his wife…

SINS OF THE PAST
by Elizabeth Power

Devastated by her lover's betrayal, Riva Singleman fled, carrying
away another secret of her own. Now Damiano D'Amico
is back—but will he discover the truth and demand what is
rightfully his?

On sale from 15th April 2011
Don't miss out!

*Available at WHSmith, Tesco, ASDA, Eason
and all good bookshops*
www.millsandboon.co.uk

MODERN

A Dark Sicilian Secret
by Jane Porter

Discovering Vittorio d'Severano's secret life, Jillian Smith's
dreams of a happy-ever-after crumbled into dust... But now
Vitt has returned—to claim the tiny son Jill has sworn to keep
from him!

The Beautiful Widow
by Helen Brooks

To pay off her late husband's debts, Toni George accepts a
position with notorious heartbreaker Steel Landry. But she's not
as immune to his potent brand of masculinity as she'd like to be...

The Ultimate Risk
by Chantelle Shaw

Seeing Lanzo di Cosimo again makes Gina Bailey's pulse race
at the memories of their heady affair. No longer a carefree
innocent, can she afford to surrender in the hope that he might
protect her, cherish her, for better or worse...?

A Night With Consequences
by Margaret Mayo

Kara Redman prides herself on keeping her relationship with
Blake Benedict purely professional—until a business trip to
Italy proves to be her undoing! But one night with her boss has
shocking consequences...

On sale from 6th May 2011
Don't miss out!

Cupcakes and Killer Heels
by Heidi Rice
Ruby Delisantro's usually in the driving seat when it comes to relationships, but after meeting Callum Westmore's bedroom eyes she's in danger of losing control and—worse—of *liking* it!

Sex, Gossip and Rock & Roll
by Nicola Marsh
Charli Chambers has *never* met someone as infuriating—or delectable!—as businessman Luca Petrelli. Can she ever get close enough to the real Luca for their fling to be more than just a one-hit wonder?

The Love Lottery
by Shirley Jump
When her name is unexpectedly drawn in the town's love lottery, uptight Sophie Watson's horrified to be matched with smug-but-sexy Harlan Jones! A week of dating him will be *terrible*—won't it?

Her Moment in the Spotlight
by Nina Harrington
Mimi Ryan's debut fashion show is her dream come true. If she's being bossy then grumpy photographer Hal Langdon will just have to live with it! It's a shame she can't get his strong arms or teasing smile out of her mind...

On sale from 6th May 2011
Don't miss out!

Available at WHSmith, Tesco, ASDA, Eason and all good bookshops

www.millsandboon.co.uk

THE QUEEN OF ROMANCE BRINGS YOU A TALE OF POWER, PASSION AND PRIDE.

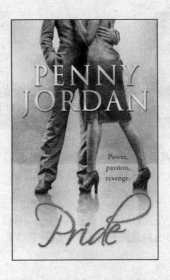

The Leopardi Brothers:
Sicilian by name...
Scandalous, scorching and seductive by nature!

Three darkly handsome Leopardi men must hunt
down the missing heir. It is their duty—as Sicilians,
as sons, as brothers! The scandal and seduction they
will leave in their wake is just the beginning...

BAD BLOOD

A POWERFUL
DYNASTY,
WHERE SECRETS
AND SCANDAL
NEVER SLEEP!

VOLUME 1 – 15th April 2011
TORTURED RAKE
by Sarah Morgan

VOLUME 2 – 6th May 2011
SHAMELESS PLAYBOY
by Caitlin Crews

VOLUME 3 – 20th May 2011
RESTLESS BILLIONAIRE
by Abby Green

VOLUME 4 – 3rd June 2011
FEARLESS MAVERICK
by Robyn Grady

8 VOLUMES IN ALL TO COLLECT!

www.millsandboon.co.uk

2 FREE BOOKS
AND A SURPRISE GIFT

We would like to take this opportunity to thank you for reading this Mills & Boon® book by offering you the chance to take TWO more specially selected books from the Modern™ series absolutely FREE! We're also making this offer to introduce you to the benefits of the Mills & Boon® Book Club™—

- **FREE home delivery**
- **FREE gifts and competitions**
- **FREE monthly Newsletter**
- **Exclusive Mills & Boon Book Club offers**
- **Books available before they're in the shops**

Accepting these FREE books and gift places you under no obligation to buy, you may cancel at any time, even after receiving your free books. Simply complete your details below and return the entire page to the address below. You don't even need a stamp!

YES Please send me 2 free Modern books and a surprise gift. I understand that unless you hear from me, I will receive 4 superb new books every month for just £3.30 each, postage and packing free. I am under no obligation to purchase any books and may cancel my subscription at any time. The free books and gift will be mine to keep in any case.

Ms/Mrs/Miss/Mr _____ Initials _____
_____
Surname _____
Address _____
_____
_____ Postcode _____
E-mail _____

Send this whole page to: Mills & Boon Book Club, Free Book Offer, FREEPOST NAT 10298, Richmond, TW9 1BR